# PEBBLES

*Sea shells*

&

# GEMSTONES

## S. CHANDRA

**BLUEROSE PUBLISHERS**
India | U.K.

Copyright © S. Chandra 2024

All rights reserved by author. No part of this publication may be reproduced, stored in a retrieval system, or transmitted in any form or by any means, electronic, mechanical, photocopying, recording or otherwise, without the prior permission of the author. Although every precaution has been taken to verify the accuracy of the information contained herein, the publisher assumes no responsibility for any errors or omissions. No liability is assumed for damages that may result from the use of information contained within.

BlueRose Publishers takes no responsibility for any damages, losses, or liabilities that may arise from the use or misuse of the information, products, or services provided in this publication.

For permissions requests or inquiries regarding this publication, please contact:

BLUEROSE PUBLISHERS
www.BlueRoseONE.com
info@bluerosepublishers.com
+91 8882 898 898
+4407342408967

ISBN: 978-93-6261-276-2

Cover design: Rishab
Typesetting: Sagar

First Edition: October 2024

# *Foreword*

Nature is indeed awe inspiring! We, the mortal beings are born into nature either by the grace of providence, or as a course of evolution, or is it the synergy of both providence and evolution? I wonder if this were true for all the species on this earth: the flora or fauna distributed all over the globe.

One is intrigued at the diversity and the panoramic view that nature provides. The universe that is profound, immeasurable and limitless. We marvel at the orbiting planets, natural satellites, the twinkling stars of the innumerable galaxies. The radiant sun that energises the Earth, The vast space, the blue skies, oceans, seas, rivers, streams, lakes, backwaters, estuaries, pools, puddles, mountains, hills, valleys, forests, glens, wetlands, ice lands, pastures, grasslands, meadows, vast fields, deserts, oases and many more that is beyond one's imagination!

All these are bejewelled with boulders, rocks, stones, gravel, grit, pebbles, shingles, sand, clay, mud, soil rich in minerals. Furthermore, nature springs into life with the flora and fauna. The flora represented by the diverse kinds of plant species viz. algae, fungi, mosses, liverworts, ferns, horsetails, birches, spruces, pines, herbs, shrubs, bushes, and trees. The majority of the flora bestowed with the uniqueness of trapping solar energy in the form of food and passing it on to the next level of the food chain. Was it chance or was it merely the process of progression that featured them to be autotrophic and being grounded to the soil?

The bewildering fauna represented by the myriad of animal species ranging from the tiny protozoa to the gigantic forms. This includes non-vertebrates the unicellular forms viz. amoebae, slipper animalcules, a host of sponges, coelenterates, bryozoans, annelids, arthropods, molluscs and echinoderms; the link species between invertebrates and the vertebrates represented by amphioxus / the lancelets, the tunicates and a few more. The vertebrates represented by the cartilaginous and bony fishes, the amphibians, the reptiles, the birds, the mammals and the most evolved human beings. Once again I wonder whether it was a probability or was it merely the process of advancement that featured them to be heterotrophic and locomotors. Indeed an admirable close-knit of inorganic and organic matter that enables the blue / green planet to pulsate with life and energy.

Why did I choose to title this book as *Pebbles, Seashells and Gemstones*? As an observer, I have always been inspired by the diversity in nature and human as well as their co-relationship. Further, I am always amazed as I admire themyriad of patterns in the variety of inanimate pebbles, seashells and gemstones in this world.

This book is a compilation of short stories that highlight personalities, well-rounded and gritty as resembling pebbles that are formed by natural processes. A few of the human personalities in these stories resemble the variety of seashells scattered on the shores of the sea.

There are yet a few people those who have lives as ornamental and lustrous as the assortment of colourful gemstones. A corollary has been drawn between natural processes and life processes that shape pebbles, seashells, gemstones and personalities as depicted in these stories. Some of these stories are inspired by of real life incidents, while others are a product of imagination and fantasy. The characters of majority of these stories are from the coastal towns and villages of India; while the others are from the deserts, plains, hills and mountainous regions of the nation. Thereby you shall find the description of villages, towns and cities along the coastline of India as well a few other regions.

At my secondary stage of schooling, I was introduced to the meaningful and thought provoking couplets by *Saint Kabir*, a weaver by profession. These couplets have not only left a deep impression in my mind but have also helped me reflect upon and imbibe the values and philosophy of life. Majority of his couplets clearly depict the true relationship between man and matter, beings and matter and living things and matter.

Reference to this popular couplet by *Sant Kabir*;

### माटी कहे कुम्हार से, तू क्या रौंदे मोहे
### एक दिन ऐसा आएगा, मैं रौंदूंगी तोहे !

**Maati kahe kumhaar se, tu kya raunde moahe,
ik din aisa aayega, mai raundoongi toahe!**

The soil (*maati*) says to the potter (*kumhaar*) why do you continue to trample (*raunde*) upon me (*moahe*)? There shall be a day (*ik din aisaaayega*) when I (*mai*) shall be trampling (*raundoongi*) you (*toahe*). In other words all mortal beings, however strong and powerful they may be shall one day be decomposed in the soil.

During my childhood, I would often hear elders telling the children that lifetime good deeds and acts help mortal men to transform to twinkling stars after their death. It could be a myth, fantasy or a figment. The Pole Star known as *Dhruwa taara* would often be cited as an example. *Dhruwa* was the son *Suniti*, the first wife of King *Uttanapad*. The King showered all his love and attention on *Uttama*, the son of his second wife *Suruchi*; whereas *Dhruwa* longed for the fatherly love that he was deprived of. Thereby, on the advice of his mother and sage *Narada*, *Dhruwa* started his incessant penance, standing on one leg in honour of *Lord Vishnu* under a *Kadamba* tree on the banks of river *Yamuna*. It is said that his indomitable faith, undeterred spirits and ardent devotion in chanting the name of Lord *Narayana'* shook the world. Consequently Lord *Narayana* appeared, consoled him and blessed him that his desires would come true. What started with seeking the attention of his father's love resulted in not only in sitting on his father's lap and ruling the kingdom but also his anointment into a Star, much above the *Saptarishis*, after he would leave the world.

I strongly believe and imagine that if the above story is true; there could be many beings and humans who transform into soulful pebbles, seashells and gemstones. Because after death, our bodies progressively decompose and transform to matter that could lay the foundation to the variety of soulful pebbles, seashells and gemstones.

I acknowledge my sincere thanks to all the people who walked into my life, all my readings plus happenings in my life. I also express my gratitude to the powerful force of the Universe that has helped me to exist on this planet as a soulful and thoughtful woman.

I appreciate and extend my gratitude to all the readers for having read my first book titled **Golden Summers** and for their reviews. I also acknowledge my gratefulness to the Publishers for facilitating the publication of my second book titled **Pebbles, Seashells and Gemstones**. Thanks to my parents, guides, counsellors and mentors who as teachers have not only stimulated me to live, to think freely and unfold all my thoughts. In the words of Maria Montessori: *'To stimulate life, leaving it then free to develop, to unfold, herein is the first task of the teacher.*

Happy reading!

**S. Chandra**

# Contents

| | |
|---|---|
| FOREWORD | iii |
| **PEBBLES** | 1 |
| A Prelude to the Stories | 2 |
| Great-Grandma's Chest of Treasures | 6 |
| The Death of a Primate | 59 |
| **SEASHELLS** | 75 |
| An Interlude to the Stories | 76 |
| He Dared To Be a Pied Piper | 81 |
| Spring Tides and Neap Tides | 93 |
| **GEMSTONES** | 123 |
| A Postlude to the Stories | 124 |
| The Solitary Septuagenarian | 129 |
| The Navaratna Pendant | 142 |

# PEBBLES

# A Prelude to the Stories

**Introduction:** I have ventured to express my thoughts, because as a member of the human society, I do think as other human beings do. We evolved as a species on this Earth between 2 million to 1.5 million BCE. Thus, when we came into existence, we were born into the wilderness with elements of nature around viz. the sky, the sun, the planets, the stars, the mountains and hills, the meadows, the pastures, the deserts and ice covered lands, the rivers, seas and oceans, plants and animals of all kinds plus all that you can imagine in nature. Thus, nature is much older than human origin and existence.

Further, we as human beings are adapted to the terrestrial habitats of the ecosystem; thereby we are termed to be terrestrial beings. Hence, we are related to the Earth, which is chiefly made up of soil and rocks. Although three-fourth of the earth is water, we as human beings are not adapted to live in water as aquatic animals do; thereby we are quite well adapted to live in terrestrial conditions. The word terrestrial is derived from the Latin word 'terra' which refers to the goddess of Earth; land itself. This prompted me to think about "rocks, boulders and stones" as the chief constituent of terrestrial ecosystem and thereby the question 'when did rocks, boulders, hills and mountains come into existence?'

According to geologists, the oldest terrestrial rocks on this Earth dates back to 4 billion years. There is yet another category of rocks that are non-terrestrial as they have been formed by the fall of meteorites. These rocks date back to 7 billion years.

As mentioned in the foreword, mortal beings are made up of matter; thereby after the death of beings, the physical body is recycled to the Earth as soil or matter through the process of decomposition. Hence I choose to dedicate the stories to the oldest forms of matter that is ROCKS!

**International Rock Day:** July 13th, every year is observed as International Rock Day, all over the biosphere. Rocks have been used by human beings over the time as human civilization began. History of human civilization records that, when two flint stones were struck together man came to know about how to create fire. Stones were used as tools, for constructing reservoirs, for architecture, for erecting structures to prevent excessive flow of water, for extracting minerals and many more reasons.

Although rocks may not seem to be very important to one but are essential for the existence, survival and advancement of mankind. Rocks may be of three kinds, igneous, sedimentary and metamorphic. Each of them is formed by many physical changes and processes that together make up the rock cycle.

Sedimentary rocks are formed from pieces of other existing rock / organic material. The three kinds of sedimentary rocks are *klastic / clastic* (fragment of rock formed due to weathering), organic (biological) and chemical (molecular properties of substances). Metamorphic rocks are of two kinds foliated and non-foliated. Both these types are formed under heat and pressure, when the original form of rock changes its form. Igneous rocks are formed from molten lava intrusive (within the magma of the earth) or extrusive (on the earth's crust)

**What are Pebbles? What accounts for their diversity?** Pebbles are small, rounded rocks that originate from rocks and stones that have been worn down (weathered) by the constant pounding of waves, tides and currents in rivers, oceans and sea beaches. The geological history, mineral composition and environmental factors have contributed to the diversity of pebbles.

Diversity includes range of shapes and colours of pebble stones. Pebbles are generally rounded or oblong shaped. Their size may vary from small to large. Colours may range from neutral tones i.e. grey, beige, and white to vibrant hues of black, blue, green, orange and red.

Erosion and weathering processes shape pebbles into round and smooth forms. Further, different rock types and their mineral compositions affect pebble shape and texture. Reference to the colour of pebbles: their mineral composition and chemical properties of the original rock account for their colour. Geological processes, including oxidation and sedimentation can alter the colour of the pebbles over a period of time.

People often wonder at the divine powers of the black *'shaligrama'* that was once upon a time a pebble. These are found till date in the sacred rivers of Himalayas and across river *Gandaki*, near *Muktinath* in Nepal. *Shaligram* Stones are fossilised ammonite (a type of mollusc that lived millions of years ago in the Cretaceous Period). Note that these pebbles are neither artificial nor man-made. They are naturally made by geological processes.

Here's a quote by Dalai Lama: *"Just as ripples spread out when a single pebble is dropped into water, the actions of individuals can have far-reaching effects."* The characters in the two stories that follow are dedicated to the wonderful world of PEBBLES.

*******************************************

# Great-Grandma's Chest of Treasures

### Part 1

<u>**Nandu** and his grandmother, **Achhamma**:</u> It was a warm summer morning. One could hear a variety of noises as the sun on the horizon, moved up from behind the hills. The tweet of the chirping birds, the gurgling waters of the stream, the jingle of the temple bells, the clippetty-clop sounds of the hooves of the cattle as they walked past the window on the cobble-stone pathway in front of the house.

The sun shone bright on *Nandu's* face, yet he was fast asleep. He lent a deaf ear to his mother's calls and his father's rebukes. Although asleep, his conscious mind reminded him that it was the first day of the summer vacation and there was no need for him to wake up early. *Ammachhi* had allowed him to oversleep by an hour, as a treat for the first day of the Christmas vacation. She got furious when *Nandu* wouldn't wake up beyond the granted hour, despite all her efforts.

She brought in a small bucket of water and threw the water from a distance with force aiming at *Nandu's* face. Splash! *Nandu* woke up quite startled. He was tempted to shout at *Amma*. However at the sight of *Achhan's* tall figure standing at the doorway, he threw off the bed-sheet that he had wrapped himself with and bolted out from the cosy corner darting to the area behind his house. He mumbled to himself expressing his displeasure on his mother's act of waking him up from a beautiful dream.

He walked to the well wherein his grandmother was busy drawing out water and pouring the drawn out water into large cement troughs.

Spotting her, *Nandu* cried with joy, "*Achamma!*"

*Achamma* in turn looked behind and responded with glee "*Nandukutta!*"

*Nandu* hugged his 65 year old paternal grandmother from behind almost tipping off her balance. She dropped the rope that was attached to a *kudam* (brass pitcher) with which she was drawing water from the well. Lo! The brass pitcher hung to the rope went slipping into the well. *Raghava*, the gardener who was nearby, pruning the full grown bushes, sprang up to rescue grandmother's brass pitcher. His jump was almost like a Superman's dive and he was successful in catching hold of a length of the rope, preventing it from further slipping down.Ten year old *Nandu* joyfully clapped his hands and shouted, "*Raghavan Chetta! What a super dive and catch! Soo.....ooo......per!*"

*Achamma* looked at *Nandu* sternly and said that she was annoyed with him for two things: first for waking up so late and second for tipping off her balance. *Nandu* held his ear lobes and said that he was sorry. However he pleaded that, since it was vacation time he should be allowed to wake up late. *Achhamma* did not yield to his pleadings and said in English imitating his *Achhan*, "Nothing doing!" *Nandu* laughed aloud listening to his grandmother uttering English in a typical *Malayalam* accent and made fun of her.

*Achamma* picked up a stick from her surrounding and started shooing *Nandu* away. *Nandu* began running about and took fun as *Achamma* continued to chase him. She kept shouting '*Azhukku Kutta! Azhukku Nandu!*' ( Dirty boy! Dirty *Nandu!*) This was because it was about 8 in the morning and he had neither brushed his teeth nor was he through his morning ablutions or bathed himself. After a five minute chase *Achamma* was successful in pushing *Nandu* into the washroom that was located in the backyard.

**Memories *Achamma* recalls her golden past:** Weary and exhausted by chasing *Nandu*.... *Achamma* sat on a chair in the backyard. Gradually she fell into a reverie, recalling moments and incidents of her lifetime.

*Achamma* alias *Indu Menon,* had retired as a Senior Matron from the Government hospital *Kovalam*. She had acquired her Nursing Degree from the Nursing College at *Kozhikode*. At the age of 22 her parents found a suitable match for her. Thus, *Indu Nair* alias *Achamma* wedded *Radhakrishnan Menon* and moved to a village named Kallada, 27 Kilometres away from *Kovalam*.

It took her quite some time to understand her husband well and get adjusted to the lifestyle in the village house. This was because she was born and thoroughly bred in the city of *Kozhikode,* popular as Calicut during the British rule. Initially, the village lifestyle intimidated her. However, her mother-in-law, *Ashalata Menon*, who was in complete charge of the house and her father-in-law, *Colonel Nandakishore Menon*, who was a retired military officer were always there to put her at ease. Both of them doted upon her as they did not have a daughter because *Radhkrishnan* was their only son.

By virtue of being the only son of his parents, her husband, *Radhakrishnan Menon* had gradually acquired from his father the knowhow and the skills of managing the *Tharavadu-* ancestral house and the vast acreage of agricultural lands. His post graduate degree in Agriculture helped him in implementing latest technologies and agricultural practices. He was a knowledgeable, busy man and quite a strict disciplinarian. He would be active from dawn to desk supervising as well as discharging a variety of jobs. He was an early bird, rising up at 4:00 a.m.

After an hour of *Yoga* and *Pranayama*, he would visit the cattle-shed feed them, talk to each one of them as well as examine them. He would then visit the pen with the poultry birds, look out for the eggs laid by them and hand them over to *Raghavan Chaeta*. By 6:30 a.m. he would be ready after his morning ablutions and bath. After his daily *Pooja* he would be ready to have his breakfast and browse through the morning newspapers. By 8:30 a.m. he would be ready to move out to supervise the work being done in the farms and agricultural lands as well as the condition of the agricultural implements, tools, tractors, threshing and winnowing machines. He also served as a part time lecturer in the Agricultural College. His practical experience and skills helped him to be very much sought to by his students.

*Raghavan Chetta* and his wife *Beena Chechhi* lived in the outhouse at the backyard. They had come along with *Ashalata*, from her hometown, when she was wedded to Colonel *Nandakishore Menon*. Both of them were taken care of very well by the *Menon* family for all the work and odd jobs that they discharged. *Raghavan* took care of all the plants around the *Tharavad*. He would often run errands for the day-to-day purchases involved and as deputed by the *Menons'*. *Beena* was responsible for keeping *Menons'* residence spick and span. Her main job was housekeeping. Thus she would always be busy with scrubbing, mopping, cleaning, washing clothes and the utensils. Although *Ashalata* was the queen of the kitchen and she would remain focused in preparing beverages viz. coffee, tea sweets, savouries, snacks and dishes for nutritious meals for the family; *Beena* assisted her in odd jobs viz. chopping vegetables, grating coconuts, cleaning and chopping fish.

**Grandparents *Ashalata* & *Nandakishore Menon* and their four grandchildren:** A year and half after her marriage, *Indu Nair* received an appointment as a nursing assistant at the government hospital at *Kovalam*. The family was quite supportive and thus she served in the field of nursing for 36 years. Although challenging, *Indu* with the support of her husband managed her family and her profession quite ably. In due course of time, the *Radhakrishnans'* were blessed with four children: two sons and two daughters. The eldest son *Manoj* was born four years after their marriage. Two years later, the couple were blessed with identical twins *Bindu* and *Sindhu*. Further, two years later *Vinod* was born.

All the four children were doted upon by their grandparents. They were fortunate to receive the guidance and attention of *Ashalata Menon* and Colonel *Nandakishore Menon*. The grandmother would not only feed them but also nurture them with morals and values from *Panchatantra* tales and stories from *Ramayana & Mahabharata*.

She would sing to them songs in praise of *Lord Krishna and Rama*, as she was quite well-versed with the *Carnatic* style of rendition of music. *Manoj, Bindu and Sindhu* would accompany their grandfather on long walks across the farm, ponds and lakes. He taught the children swimming, cycling, and climbing up trees and mountains. At times grandfather would carry *Vinod* on his shoulders during such trips.

Although both the parents *Indu* and *Radhakrishnan* were very busy with their occupation; they would always find time to speak to the children, play with them, and monitor their academic progress at school. On Saturday evenings, festivals and birthdays of their children they made it a point to visit the village temple. The children would be periodically taken to the beachside. At times they visited their relatives in the neighbouring villages. Thus the closely knit family lived together leading a peaceful and content life.

**Eldest grandson *Manoj*'s passion, leads him to the skies:** Colonel *Nandakishore Menon* proved to be a role model for his grandson, *Manoj* who was greatly inspired by the war stories that his grandfather often narrated to him. When he had completed Class V, he qualified the *Sainik School* entrance examination and thereby studied from Class VI to XII at the residential *Sainik School* at *Kazhakoottam*. Later he qualified the exams that provided him an entry into the National Defence Academy, *Khadakwasla, Pune*. Subsequent to completion of three years at NDA, *Manoj* joined the Indian Air Force Academy located at *Dundigal,* on the *Medak-Hyderabad* Road. Soon after completion of rigorous training for Flying and Ground duty for a year and half he was commissioned as a Flying Officer. He gradually made a mark as Flight Lieutenant; then as a Squadron Leader, posted at *New Delhi*.

***Ashalata &Nandkishore* become great-grandparents while *Indu & Radhakrishnan* become grandparents:** *Manoj* was serving as a Flying Officer. Once during his home visit, he was betrothed to *Lavanya* who was serving as a Mathematics Teacher at the *Kendriya Vidyalaya, Kollam*. They were wedded after a year. *Lavanya* preferred to continue her services at the school. Thereby she would come down during weekends to stay at *Kallada,* the native village of her in-laws' wherein her husband *Manoj* would periodically visit.

In four years time*Manoj* and *Lavanya* were first blessed with a son, who was named *Vipin* andthree years later, a daughter, who was named as *Shailaja*. Both the children went into a local preschool. Thus *Indu & Radhakrishnan* were greatly delighted to be first addressed as *Achhamma & Achhappa* by their grandchildren *Vipin and Shailaja*. So were the great-grandparents, *Ashalata and Nandakishore* to be first addressed as *Mutthacchi & Mutthachhan!*

As soon as each one of her children turned six years old; *Lavanya* ensured that each one of them was enrolled into the *Kendriya Vidyalaya* where she served. Thereby, *Lavanya's* weekend visits to her in-laws' place at *Kallada* became infrequent. *Manoj* made it a point to be with his parents at least twice a year during his official leave. He ensured that one of his official leave period, coincided with his children's school vacation, which helped him to bring along his wife and children to stay with his parents and grandparents for a period of three to four weeks.

**Growth of *Manoj's* twin sisters *Bindu and Sindhu*):** Meanwhile *Indu & Radhakrishnan's* twin daughters *Bindu and Sindhu* grew up under the guidance and tutelage of her grandparents and parents. Both were quite sharp and intelligent. They were also easy going, fun loving and cheerful. Taking advantage of their 'look-alike' faces and identical features; they loved to play pranks with their school friends and many a time with *Raghavan Chaetta* and *Beena Chaechi*. They were initially enrolled in a local *Malayalam* medium elementary school. Both of them attended the afternoon *Carnatic* Music and *Bharatnatyam* Dance classes. Later they shifted to the local government high school wherein they could learn English and *Hindi* in addition to *Malayalam*.

Later, *Bindu and Sindhu* graduated from Government College *Kanjiramkulam*. *Bindu* pursued her courses in Commerce, while *Sindhu* opted for Fine Arts. A year later *Bindu* was fortunate enough to clear a qualifying examination that provided her an entry into the *Canara Bank* at *Kovalam*. *Sindhu* was passionate with Fine Arts, thereby in due course of time she was absorbed as a faculty at the College of Fine Arts at *Thiruvanathapuram*.

**Pivotal efforts of the *Menon* grandparents in negotiating the marriage of their twin grand-daughters:** Both the grandparents were keen to get *Bindu and Sindhu* married off at a right age. Thereby *Nandakishore Menon* started searching for suitable alliances through the community marriage brokers and matrimonial columns in leading dailies. One Friday evening *Nandakishore Menon* summoned his wife, *Ashalata* his son, *Radhakrishnan* and daughter-in-law, *Indu* to the *koodam* (central hall) and brief them about all the proposals received and help him select three suitable matches each for *Bindu and Sindhu*.

After thorough scrutiny of all the available proposals, debate and deliberations; *Radhakrishnan Menon* and his wife, *Indu* managed to pick six suitable prospective candidates. When they presented these alliances to their daughters for their opinion and choice; *Bindu* said that she would be content with her parents' choice whereas *Sindhu* wanted *Bindu*'s opinion on her parents' choice of a suitable match. In a month's time after a series of processes and negotiations, the wedding ceremony of both the sisters was solemnized at the village temple with a grand reception at the village community hall. Thus, when *Bindu* and *Sindhu*got married they were 25 years of age.

**_Bindu_ and _Sindhu_ move out from their birth place to get settled with their respective life partners:** *Bindu's* husband, *Santhosh* was an executive at the Life Insurance Corporation of India, *Chennai*. The family hailed from *Thrissur*. His father was a general physician in the government hospital whereas his mother was a homemaker. His younger sister and younger brother were pursuing their college studies at *Thrissur*.

*Bindu* continued to serve in the bank at *Kovalam*. She occasionally would be with her in-laws at *Thrissur*, especially when *Santosh* would come down from *Chennai*. Initially, it was quite tedious for her commuting to and fro and thereby she contemplated on quitting the job. Meanwhile, she had also applied for a transfer to *Chennai* which materialized three months after her wedding. Thus she moved to *Chennai* and started living with her husband. In due course of time *Bindu* and *Santhosh* were blessed with two daughters. The elder daughter, *Rituja* was born two years after their wedding. When *Rituja* was three years old, her sibling *Jalaja* was born.

*Sindhu's* husband, *Kartik-Vijay* was a Computer software engineer working with Oracle at Technopark at *Thiruvananthapuram / Tririvandrum*. He was the only son of a businessman, an authorized dealer and distributor of automobile parts. His mother was a registered homeopath, practising for the past 18 years. After her wedding, *Sindhu* moved to the residence of *Kartik-Vijay* and started living with her husband and in-laws'.

*Sindhu's* father-in-law would be round the clock busy with his business. Her mother-in-law's clinic was functional from 10:30 a.m. to 1:30 p.m. and 4:30 p.m. to 6:30 p.m. It would always have a beeline of patients. *Sindhu's* college timings were from 9:30 a.m. to 4:00 p.m. Thereby her husband would drop her at the College and move to his office at 10:00 a.m. He would generally return after 7:00 p.m. Thereby the entire family would spend time together on Saturday evenings and go for an outing on Sundays. *Sindhu* and *Karthik-Vijay* were blessed with a son, four years after their marriage. He was named as *Kartik-Vignesh*.

**Career pursuit of *Vinod*, the youngest grandson of *Ashalata* & *Nandakishore Menon*:** *Vinod*, the youngest son of *Indu and Radhakrishnan*, was a trained classical singer in *Carnatic Music*. He participated in Music festivals and concerts in the temple and various other platforms in the village. His shows gradually gained popularity and he had quite a large fan following. *Vinod* who was two years younger to *Bindu and Sindhu*, followed his sister *Bindu Chaechi's* footsteps and completed his graduation in Commerce, pursued his studies further to become a Chartered Accountant. He established his office at the outskirts of the village. He had two partners with him. His job as a Certified Auditor also earned him a good clientele and reputation. He also had quite a few CA aspirants who sought guidance from him.

*Vinod* met *Sarita* at a music concert at *Shri Krishna Gana Sabha, Chennai. Sarita* was an accomplished instrumentalist. She played the violin in the *Carnatic* style of music. She was a certified *Akashvani*, All India Radio artiste and worked at AIR *Thiruvanathapuram.* It was a case of 'love at first sight' for *Vinod* and *Sarita*. After a year of clandestine courtship; *Vinod* and *Sarita* got married, with the approval of their parents. A year after their wedding *Mythili* was born bringing yet another opportunity of happiness and rejoicement for the great-grandparents *Ashalata Menon and Nandakishore Menon* and grandparents *Indu Menon* and *Radhkrishnan Menon. Nandu* was born to *Vinod* and *Sarita*, two years later.

**Great-grandparents set out for a pilgrimage:** Soon after the birth of *Mythili, Ashalata Menon and Nandakishore Menon* planned a three week '*kshetradanam*' i.e. a trip to various temples in the southern region. *Raghavan chaeta* and his tourist guide nephew, *Krishnankutty* accompanied them. *Radhakrishnan Menon,* was not very keen that his mother who was 85 years old, and his father who was 89 years old, take this trip in the month of December as it was quite cold. Further he was apprehensive as he could not accompany them. However, he could not, in any possible way, dissuade his parents, thereby he had to reluctantly yield to his parents' desire for this pilgrimage tour.

In consonance with his parents, *Radhakrishnan* chalked out the itinerary and made all the bookings and reservations for the travel: onward journey to different destinations as well as arrangement through suitable contacts, for their lodging and boarding at suitable hotels and guest houses as well as their return journey. He solely depended on the prudence *Raghavan chaeta* and *Raghavan's* nephew.

*Ashalata Menon and Nandakishore Menon* started their journey along with *Raghavan* and *Krishnankutty*on the 30$^{th}$ of November of the year.

- ➢ They first visited the *Ananta Padmanabhaswamy* temple at *Thiruvanathapuram*. Although they had visited the temple several times, there was always something new at the temple that mesmerized them during their visits. After a four day stay at the capital city of *Kerala*, they proceeded by train to the next destination *Kanyakumari*.

- ➢ The visit to the 3000 year old *Bhagavathy Kanyakumari* temple was indeed invigorating. The couple enjoyed watching the hues of colours in the horizon during sunrise and sunset and the communion of the three colours of waters at the confluence of Bay of Bengal, Indian Ocean and the Arabian Sea. They often lost track of time sitting on the beach watching the tides, sands scattered with seashells as the tides receded. They purchased from the local shops articles made out of sea-shells in addition to large shells one each engraved with the names of every family member. Another favourite spot which the couple loved to visit was the Vivekananda Rock Memorial temple.

After a four day stay at *Kanyakumari* the next destination was *Rameshwaram*.

➤ On the first day during sunrise at *Rameshwaram*, the couple had the holy dip in *Agnitheertham*. They also visited the *Ramantahaswamy* temple dedicated to Lord Shiva. The visit to *Rama Sethu* and *Pamaban Bridge* was indeed a rewarding experience for the couple. The four day stay at *Rameshwaram*, offered an exhilarating experience for the octogenarian couple.

➤ As per the itinerary the next destination was *Madurai*. During their four day stay at *Madurai*, they were greatly impressed to see the grandeur of the 12$^{th}$ century architectural marvel constructed by the *Pandiyan* Kings; the *Madurai Meenakshi Temple*, especially the *gopuram* of all the entrance doors, the large doorways, the corridors and the richness of the sculptures on every pillar and wall. The couple were mesmerised with the beauty of the deity Goddess *Meenakshi* with the parrot in one of her hands. They also visited the *Azhagar* Temple, *MariammanTheppakulam* and *Subramaniya Swami* temple.

➤ The last destination was *Guruvayur* also known as the *Dwaraka* of the South and the *Bhooloka Vaikuntham*. The 5000 year old ancient temple has a history wherein *Lord Krishna* set his charioteer *Udhava* on a mission to save the idol of *Vishnu* worshipped by him in *Dwaraka*. The charioteer invoked the *Guru*, the Teacher of the Gods and *Vayu*, the Lord of Winds and was successful in transporting the idol from *Dwaraka* to *Guruvayur* a district of *Thrissur*.

*Krishnankutty* and *Raghavan chaeta* were of a great help to the *Menons*. They served as knights, sentries and the best of aides. It was their duty to telephonically call up *Radhakrishnan*, from available STD (Subscribers' Trunk Dialling System) Booth, soon after they reached a destination. The purpose was to keep him informed about the welfare of *Ashalata* and *Nandakishore Menon*.

**The octogenarians return home after three weeks of pilgrimage:** On 22$^{nd}$ December of the year, the great-grandparents returned home after completing the *kshetradanam*. The anxious son, *Radhakrishnan Menon* was very relieved to see his parents hale and hearty, and rejuvenated. He and his wife were waiting at the entrance of the *tharavadu* to receive them. They touched their feet and received their blessings. *Radhakrishnan* embraced *Raghavan Chaeta*, shook hands with *Krishnankutty* and thanked both of them profusely for not only escorting his parents on pilgrimage but for also have taken care of them so very well throughout the journey.

*Ashalata & Nandakishore* were happy to be at home, especially to see all the grandchildren and great-grandchildren assembled at their residence. They realised that Christmas was round the corner. It was winter vacation time for all the school children. Schools were to reopen on the 2<sup>nd</sup> of January, the next year. Thereby, the four children of *Radhakrishnan & Indu Menon's* viz. *Manoj, Bindu, Sindhu and Vinod* decided to bring along their children for a week to stay along with their great-grandparents and grandparents in their ancestral home at the village.

**Close-knit family and fun-time for the seven cousins:** On the previous day of the arrival of the great-grandparents from the pilgrimage; family of *Manoj* and *Lavanya* had arrived followed by *Vinod* and *Sarita*; *Sindhu* and *Kartik-Vijay* as well as *Bindu* and *Santosh*. The seven cousins danced with glee to meet after almost a year. *Muthhachhan* addressed them collectively as *Saptaswarangal* (the seven musical notes).

*Vipin* and *Shailaja* were 16 and 13 years of age respectively. *Rituja* and *Jalaja* were 14 and 11 years by age. *Kartik-Vignesh* was 8 years old and *Mythili* and *Nandu* were 12 and 10 years old.

Thus, in an ascending order of ages the youngest of the *Saptaswarangal* was *Karthik-Vignesh* < *Nandu* < *Jalaja* < *Mythili* < *Shailaja* < *Rituja* < *Vipin* being the eldest of the cousins. The teenagers *Vipin, Rituja* and *Shailaja*, many a time would separate out from the group as they felt that *Karthik-Vignesh, Nandu, Jalaja and Mythili* were prying and childish.

*Part 2*

**_Achhamma_ alias _Indu_ wakes up with a start from her reverie:** *Achhamma* woke up with a start, when she was shaken up by her grand-daughter, *Mythili*, who had found her grandmother on the chair in the backyard, sitting still in a trance, with her eyes closed.

*Nandu* had come out from the washroom long back. He found his grandmother sitting motionless in the chair in the backyard and was not responding to his calls; he rushed in dragged out his elder sister, *Mythili*. Fearing something was wrong with *Achhamma*, she cried out, in her shrill voice, "*Achhamma!*", "*Achhamma!*"

Listening to the cries of *Nandu* and *Mythili*; *Sarita* and *Vinod*, their *Amma* and *Achhan* rushed out. *Achamma* was embarrassed that she had fallen into a trance that transported her to the past, recalling majority of the events of her life over the last six decades.

She gradually managed to convince her anxious son and daughter-in-law that nothing was wrong with her. She moved inwards to the large spacious kitchen and found *Beena chaechi*, *Lavanya*, *Bindu* and *Sindhu* busy preparing the elaborate three course lunch. *Achhamma* also joined them to help in the process.

**Vacation delight- fun and frolic time:** All throughout the eight day stay in the village; *Manoj*, *Santosh* and *Kartik-Vijay* preferred to stay indoors or in the nature, seeking a break from the hubbub of the city life that they were accustomed to. The children enjoyed to explore every nook and corner of the ancestral house. In the forenoon, *Radhakrishnan* would take them out to the backwater jetty, farms and fields. Children enjoyed exploring, climbing up trees, chasing butterflies, and tractor rides, boat and steamer rides. *Vipin* ventured into driving the tractors and was elated with hisendeavour. They were accosted by almost everyone who met them on the way. They were amazed to know how popular their grandfather, *Radhkrishnan Menon* was in this village and beyond.

One day, in the forenoon, grandfather along with his youngest son, *Vinod* took all the seven cousins to *Kovalam* city by his Bolero SUV. The children had lots of enjoyment, singing and being merry throughout the way to the town. They went to the following places: *Neyyar Dam, Kerala Arts and Crafts Village, Oriental Arts Emporium* and *Kovalam Beach*.

**Family time:** Grandfather had planned out all the evenings quitewell, involving the entire family. An evening visit to the village temple, the next followed by a visit to the Christmas fair organised by the local church authorities along with a stage show; *Carnatic* music concert at home by *Vinod, Bindu, Sindhu, Sarita, Ashalata and Radhakrishnan.*

One evening as all the elders sat around a bonfire; all the seven children took charge and presented a live variety entertainment programme that included mimicry, a comedy show, fancy dress, dance performance, film songs and magic show. The concluding item was a musical ensemble; wherein *Vipin* and *Shailaja* were on the keyboard, *Rituja* played the flute, *Jalaja* was on the Spanish guitar, *Kartik*-Vijai on the Congo, *Mythili* and *Nandu* played the mouth organ.

*Vinod*, although a vocalist, had a passion for collecting and playing various musical instruments. He had developed a separate hall in the *tharavadu* and had beautifully arranged these instruments along with traditional ones viz. *shruti*-box, harmonium, *tanpura*, *veena*, flute, violin, *mridangam*, *tabla*, *dhagga*, *thavil* and saxophone.

The children were thus blessed to try out a few instruments and performed. *Muthacchhan* and *Muthacchhi* were thrilled to see the talents of their great-grandchildren. All the adults were mesmerized by the performance by the cousins, aptly named as *Saptaswarangal* by *Muthacchan*.

**Exploration:** On the penultimate day of their departure, in the afternoon hours, when all the adults were enjoying their afternoon siesta; the cousins managed to sneak into the hall, upstairs. *Vipin* was the leader and he led the remaining via the narrow wooden staircase made of teakwood. The children were curious to know and find out what was there in the hall. At the entrance door of the hall was a black cat with four kittens. The cat snarled at them. *Vipin* managed to shoo away the cat with its brood. The afternoon sunrays that entered into the room through the ventilator provided ample light for the children to find their way.

*Vipin* and *Rituja* tried their hands to unlatch the brass al-drop latch set at the door and found it quite difficult. Four of them applied all their might and they were able to set free the latch. The teak doors opened into the hall with a resounding creaking noise. *Nandu* and *Kartik-Vignesh* were asked to stand at the doorway to warn the others, in case an adult of the house walked up. The children were amazed to see such a big hall with large windows on the wall. All the window shutters were closed casting a gloomy look. They maintained a hush-hush silence and walked about on tip-toes lest they would wake up the adults downstairs. *Vipin* spotted a switch board with six brass switch points. He tried clicking on the switch points. One of them lit a low voltage bulb hanging from the central wooden beam of the ceiling.

There were many things that were not much in use, kept in this hall. The ceiling was low made up of strong wooden beams that ran criss-cross. The roof was made up of brick-tiles and thatches. Thus the large hall functioned as a storehouse. On the walls were large framed paintings and quite many black and white photographs. In a corner were half a dozen carpet rolls, lamp-stands, cane armchairs and tables. On another corner was a large vintage model standing pendulum clock.

Alongside a wall were five huge walnut cupboards; each one of them was locked. Along the wall opposite to these cupboards were two huge ornamentally designed wooden mahogany chests. The children had seen the picture of a similar chest in their English text-book of

Class II in a lesson titled, '*The Royal Chest of Treasures*'. Both the chests were locked with equally huge padlocks. The children were curious to know about what treasures were stored inside these chests? Meanwhile *Mythili* spotted a brass plate on the lid of the chest with the inscription **ASHALATA MENON.** There was a similar inscription on the other chest as well.

"*It's Great Grandmother's Chest of Treasures!*" the girls shouted in a chorus. The boys affirmed and said, "*Yes, the name label is the evidence that both are Muthacchhi's Chests of Treasures!*"

The children had many a time overheard their parents mentioning that they were told by *Achhamma*, about her mother-in-law being very secretive about the wealth and treasures that she had brought from her father's home in the chests that she found always locked. Further, she had never revealed / disclosed to anyone about the possessions in the chest.

"*Where could the keys of these chests be?*" all wondered. There was an open shelf with five racks. Each rack had a pair of gunny-sacks full of things. One rack at the centre had four smaller wooden boxes with sliding lids. *Vipin*, *Shailaja* and *Rituja* were bent upon in finding the keys. Thereby they opened the lids by sliding them out and rummaged through them. One had lots of metal rings / valves, rods, screws, nuts and bolts. The other box had iron nails of different sizes. The third box had rivets. The fourth one had tools viz, measuring tape, screw drivers, spanners, pliers, two screw-gauges and a vernier-caliper.

Alas! There was no object resembling the keys to the chest. Meanwhile *Nandu* and *Kartik-Vignesh* moved from their posts as both of them had spotted in a corner; a wooden rocking horse, a wooden rocking swan, a tricycle and a bicycle. *Nandu* sat on the rocking horse, while *Kartik-Vignesh* tried ringing the manual bell on the handlebar of the bicycle. It went off jingling "*Trinnnn,,,gggg!*"

*Vipin* shouted at him, "*Quiet!...... Quiet! You are going to wake up every one!*"

This was when they heard the chirp of the gecko on the wall. All were initially scared but were later amused.

Yet at another corner in a triangular closet with glass doors; there were large brass plates, brass lamps, brass pitchers and pots. On the wall beside the entrance door was hung a pair of rifles and the face of a stuffed stag.

The children got tired of their venture; however were happy that their mission was not totally fruitless. During their earlier visits, they had never thought of exploring this area. They could not contain their curiosity. Therefore, they decided that they should directly approach *Muthacchhi* and *Mutthachhan* and express their desire of seeing things in the two chests that bore the name label of **ASHALATA MENON**, their great grandmother.

*Vipin*, *Rituja* and *Shailaja* took the responsibility of switching off the bulb, setting things right, as they were previously kept and bolting the heavy al-drop latch on the door that appeared to be a Herculean task. They stealthily climbed down the narrow wooden staircase.

**The secret mission of the cousins revealed to the elders of the *Menon* family:** The children were taken aback to see their grandfather, *Radhakrishnan Menon* standing tall in the hall. It appeared as though he was waiting for the children. He appeared to be tight-lipped and wore a frown on his face. Surely, he was annoyed that the children had ventured into stepping into the area that was out of bounds for them.

He literally roared at *Vipin* and rebuked him. He said that he had least expected of him to lead his cousins, in the venture to explore the area that the children were not allowed to move to. Seeing their grandfather annoyed, all the children hung their heads down. *Jalaja* and *Mythili* trembled with fear. Listening to *Achhappan*'s loud voice, all the others who were enjoying their midday slumber woke up and walked to the hall one after the other. *Manoj & Vinod* tried to figure out whatever must have happened. They had never seen their father so furious; thereby *Manoj* shouted at *Vipin*; *Sarita* and *Vinod* raised their hands to spank *Mythili* and *Nandu*.

Watching this development *Rituja* and *Jalaja* cried out at their maternal uncles and aunts, "*Mama! Mami! Please don't punish them. All of us wanted to explore the hall upstairs, if that's a big mistake punish all of us!*" *Bindu* and *Santosh* were taken aback by their daughters' defensive statement especially at their audacity of questioning if it were a big mistake to explore the hall upstairs?

Great-grandfather, *Nandakishore Menon* who was having a nap on the recliner, woke up and intervened by asking

*Radhakrishnan* and others to maintain their cool. He summoned *Nandu* and *Kartik-Vignesh* and asked them about the entire episode. They promptly marrated that all of them had never been upstairs thereby were curious to know what was there upstairs. Further, *Beena Chaechi* and *Raghavan Chaeta* had always narrated to them stories stating that children were prohibited to go upstairs because *kuttichaattan* (little satanic ghosts), vampire bats, evil black cats and poisonous snakes lived there and would harm them if they spotted children. They candidly remarked that although they could spot a black cat with four kittens, however could not find the bats or *kuttichaattan*.

They asked, "*Mutacchha! Are there snakes guarding the treasures inside Muttacchhi's huge big trunks that are locked?*"

Listening to the innocent question by the young boys, great-grandfather started laughing aloud! His resounding laughter eased the situation and brought a smile on everyone's face including his son, *Radhakrishnan*. He realized that his grandchildren were not only curious but also were smart enough to explore whether statements and stories by elders were just cock and bull stories or was there some truth behind them. He also could make out a big difference between the two generations of his children and his grandchildren. The former generation generally accepted the statements especially those that prohibited them against certain acts in light of their safety and security. They seldom questioned their elders / parents and thereby were regarded as obedient and respectful. The latter generation on the other hand were logically guided and thereby would prefer to explore for themselves and break boundaries. At this juncture, realizing that great-grandfather was in a lighter mood, all the children thronged around him and made a request;

*"Muttachha........! Muttachha! Could you please get Muttacchi's chest of treasures opened? We are keen to see the treasures. Please, Muttaccha!*

*Saptaswarangal* cousins pleaded the same in a chorus!

After a while, *Muttachhan* yielded to the children's request and asked them to first seek *Muttacchi's* permission, as it was her possession. The children bustled into the next hall.

At the centre of the hall was a teak wood plank *Oonjaal* (swing) held by four beautifully designed sturdy metallic chains that hung from hooks on the ceiling beam, *Muttachhi* was reclining on the swing enjoying the forty winks of sleep. Thereby she was oblivious to all the happenings. She woke up to the clamour raised by the cousins and was initially confused.

*Muttachhan* and *Radhakrishnan* entered the hall and briefed *Muttacchhi* about the children's venture exploring the hall upstairs. *Muttachhan* said, *"Asha, the children are curious to know what is stored in both the boxes? Do you remember that sixty-seven years ago, when you were 18 and married to me, you had brought along the huge twin wooden chests from your home?"*

*Muttacchhi* was thoughtful for a moment and said, *"It's been a long time since I have opened those chests. I do not recall where the keys are?"* She addressed *Radhakrishnan* and said, *"Moane (Son) Radhakrishna, do you remember that ten years ago, I had asked you and Raghavan Chaeta to shift the chests upstairs? After that since I had never been able to climb the wooden staircase; thereby I never opened the chests since then."*

*"Uvvu Amme!" Radhakrishnan* replied in affirmative.

*"Didn't I hand over the keys of both the chests to you then?"*

*"Alla Amme!" Radhakrishnan* replied in negative.

She then summoned *Raghavan Chaeta* to help her recall, trace and locate the keys. Thus began a mad hunt for the keys. As he was searching for the keys in the places that he could possibly find them; *Nandakishore Menon* kept mentioning about the lack of army discipline in keeping things at the right place. *Ashalata Menon* expressed her irritation and frustration at him and asked him to stop grumbling. *Radhakrishnan, Indu, Raghavan Chaeta* and *Beena Chaechi* all were in a spree to search in different places and locate the keys, but all the efforts went in vain.

*Muttachhan* then asked, *"Where are the duplicate keys? There should be a duplicate to both the keys isn't it?"* *Muttacchhi* replied that all the four keys were in the same ring; the original pair and the duplicate pair. Exasperated, *Muttachan* on a cynical note recited the lines of a poem:

*For Want of a Nail*

*For want of a nail the shoe was lost.*
*For want of a shoe the horse was lost.*
*For want of a horse the rider was lost.*
*For want of a rider the message was lost.*
*For want of a message the battle was lost.*
*For want of a battle the kingdom was lost.*
*And all for the want of a horseshoe nail!*

Meanwhile the children were getting desperate and were eagerly waiting for the elders to locate the keys. Each one expressed his / her imagination of the treasures concealed in the chests.

To *Muttacchi's* utter dismay, *Raghavan Chaeta* questioned, *"Can't we break the locks?"*

*Muttacchi said, "Nothing doing! Raghava! How dare you talk about breaking the locks? Do you know that my father had got them specially made from Aligarh? Have patience. We shall soon find the keys!"*

**Back to Square One:** 31$^{st}$ December of the year was the last day of stay for the children in the vacation. Neither, the keys to the chest could be found, nor did great-grandmother grant permission to break open the locks of the chest, *Muttachhi* asked the children to be patient.

She promised that the age-old chests would be opened only when all the seven of them would arrive and stay together at the *tharavadu* during summer vacation, next year. The children were initially dejected, however got busy with their packing and preparation for their travel to their respective destinations. *Muttacchi* and *Acchamma* were tearful and emotional when all of them departed. They had to be content with the phone calls that they would occasionally receive from their sons, daughters and daughters-in-law and occasional visits by some of the family members who resided in *Kovalam* and *Thiruvanathapuram*.

### Part 3

<u>January *Makara- Vilakku* Festival</u>: Every year on $14^{th}$ / $15^{th}$ of January (in leap years) is marked by festivities all over India ad as well as in Kerala. Its literal translation is Capricorn Festival. Generally known as *Makara Sankranti*, this occasion marks the transition of the Sun from the Zodiac of Sagittarius (*Dhanu*) to Capricorn (*Makara*). Thereby people have a holy dip / bath in the rivers and make offerings to the Sun God as the sun begins its ascent from the south to the north. In majority of the states in India, this festival marks harvest festival.

January was always a busy month for the *Menons* both at the *tharavadu* as well as in their farmland and fields. Being the President of the *Ambalam* (temple) Committee of the village, *Radhakrishnan Menon*, along with his committee members was responsible for the planning, organization, crowd management and smooth conduct of all the week long festivities (beginning from $14^{th}$ / $15^{th}$ January) of the annual *Sastha* / *Ayyappa* Pooja, wherein *Ayyappan* the deity of *Sabarimala* is worshipped. The significant event of this occasion is the lighting of the

*Makara Jyothi* and the innumerable oil lamps (*vilakku*) on the *Sankaranti* at dusk.

*Ashalata Menon, Indu Menon, Nandakishore Menon* were also quite busy from dawn to dusk. *Muttacchan* would be busy with the daily / *NityaPooja* at home which involved 7 cycles of repetitive chanting of *Ayyappanaamam*.

All the cows in the cowshed would be given a proper bath. The ladies of the house would perform *Gopooja / gowpooja (Gow / Go*= Cow + *Pooja*= worship) by applying turmeric and vermillion on its forehead and offering them jiggery, sugar cane and plantains. The ladies would ensure that whatever was cooked was *sattvik* (pure, without any contamination). Here are some dishes offered to the Lord as an offering / *naivedyam* (before being consumed by family members) viz. *Ellurunda* (balls / *laddus* made of seasame seeds and jaggery), *Aravanapayasam* (sweet delicacy made of parboiled red rice fried in large quantities of ghee, jaggery, dried ginger and coconut pieces), *Neiappam* (pounded rice well mixed with jaggery, cardamom powder and banana to form a semi-liquid batter fried in ghee as swollen discs), *pazhampori* (bananafritters) would be offered. The diet consumed by all in the family was *sattvika bhojana* wherein consumption of fish, meat and addictive substances were restricted. Rice would be consumed, once a day. Visit to the temples during dawn and dusk was a regular feature.

In the evening, renowned *Theyyam artistes* would perform open-air theatrical traditional ritualistic dance, *Theyyam*, form native to Kerala, symbolising age old customs, traditions and beliefs especially as ancestor worship. The central dancer with heavy folk painting in red on the face and an elaborately designed head gear would dance, sing and dramatize mythological themes based on stories of *Bhagawati, Shiva, Vishnu* and many more. The rhythm and tempo would be set by the drummers.

**Postal Services and Tele-communication system:** This was the period when cell-phones / mobile phoneswere not launched in India. Tele-communication system was not advanced. Thereby the *Menons'* longed for the postman to deliver letters addressed to the Menons' by *Manoj, Bindu, Sindhu and Sarita* from their respective towns / cities. *Vinod* would go to *Trivandrum* to meet his wife and children every fortnight. Thereby he would carry the latest messages from his wife, *Sarita* and children *Mythili* and *Nandu* who were now studying in a private school in the city. Once in a while, on Saturdays / Sundays the great-grandparents' and grandparents' would be overwhelmed to receive telephone calls on their BSNL landline through STD from the grandchildren.

The grandchildren had not stopped thinking about their great-grandmother's chest of treasures or the lost keys. Once, *Jalaja* and *Mythili* had sent them a painting and a pencil drawing respectively depicting the closed chests as they had seen it and the open chests out of their imagination.

The elders viz. *Manoj, Shailaja, Bindu, Santosh. Sindhu, Kartik-Vijay, Vinod* and *Sarita* were not so keen in talking about or finding about *Muttachhi's* chest; however they wondered why were their children so obsessed with their great grandmother's possessions locked in her chest?

Time flew past with different festivals and village fairs being organised in the month of February and March. Since the keys to the chests were not traceable, anywhere at home, *Ashalata Menon* had entrusted her son *Radhakrishnan Menon* with the responsibility of getting the duplicate keys of the chest made as soon as possible. His wife *Indu* also reminded him a few times. *Radhakrishnan* had asked *RaghavanChaeta* to find out about the availability of skilled locksmiths in the vicinity or in the city. Somehow things got delayed as there were none in the village and once when, he had been to *Rashid* the locksmith at *Kovalam*; he was not available in station and would arrive only in the first week of April.

**A fresh set of duplicate keys for great grand-mother's chest made available:** *Radhakrishnan* brought in *Rashid* the locksmith from *Kovalam* to his place on the 3$^{rd}$ of April and showed him the locks on the teakwood chests. *Rashid* was a veteran in making keys for unlocking locks that would not open.

On 12$^{th}$ of April he was ready with the keys and handed them over to *Radhakrishnan*. He in turn handed over the newly made keys to his mother in the evening. She placed them at the feet of *Lord Krishna* in her *Pooja* altar. Since it was quite tedious for *Muthacchi* to mount the narrow wooden stairway leading upstairs, it was decided that with the help of four to six workers, both the chests would be brought down to *Mutthacchi* & *Mutthachhan's* hall by the afternoon of 13th April. The family was also busy planning for the *Vishukkani* festival on the subsequent day i.e. the 14th April, marking the New Year for people of Kerala.

***Vishukkani* Festival:** At the dawn of 14th April, *Nandakishore Menon* and *Radhakrishnan Menon* woke up early as usual. After an hour of Yoga and meditation, they went out for the morning walk for about an hour. For the past decade, the son accompanied his father for Yoga, meditation and morning walks. On return *Indu* would serve each one of them *kattanchaaya* (black tea). *Radhakrishnan* then would go down a few steps to the *puzha* (water body) in the backyard. He would swim and have his bath in the pond, while his father, off-late (on account of his age) avoided having bath in open water bodies; instead he had his bath in the washroom in the backyard.

Both father and son entered the *Pooja* Room together to offer their morning prayers. *Indu* and *Baena Chaechi* were responsible for keeping the *Pooja* altar spotless clean. The two and half feet brass idol of *LordKrishna* in his standing posture with flute in his hands, beautifully decorated with the garland of *thulasi* leaves/sacred basil was the centre of attraction. In the altar, in addition to a smaller brass idol of *Ganesha,* were many other lithographic paintings of various deities' viz. *Pattabhiraman-* Lord Rama with his consort *Seeta* and brother *Lakshmana* and *Hanuman, Shiva & Parvati* with their sons *Ganesha* and *Kartikeya*, *BhagawatiAmmman*, *Durga*, *Lakshmi and Saraswati*, *Guruvayur* and *Lord Ayyapa*.

*Raghavan Chaeta* would daily in the morning pluck flowers from the garden in the house. He was responsible for collecting the flowers in the basket to facilitate *Muttthacchan* and *Radhakrishnan* to perform the *archana* floral offerings). *Indu* anointed each deity with sandalwood paste and vermilion on the forehead and decorated them with flowers. The entire altar was decorated with *Cassiafistula //* Indian laburnum twigs having bunches of yellow flowers also known as *Vishukkani*. The tall brass lamp *panchamukhadeepam* (five wicks) would be lit along with fragrant incense sticks contributing to the sense of divinity and spirituality in the atmosphere. On such special occasions the *poornakalasham* (water filled copper or brass pot marked with *swastika*symbolusing turmeric paste, with mango leaves and a coconut) was placed, along with a *parra* (barrel like container) filled with husked rice grains and ears of paddy. A *thaambaalam* (large brass plate) decorated with fruits, dry fruits, currency notes and coins and small bowls of cereals, millets and pulses in front of a mirror (that could cast the reflection of everything that was placed on the plate) was also kept in front of *Lord Krishna*.

This year, on this occasion on the *thaambala*man additional wooden box with the newly prepared set of keys to the chest was kept. The *poornakalasham*, the *parra* and the decorated *thaambalam* with the mirror symbolised prayers for abundance, prosperity and bountifulness throughout the year. .

***Mutthacchi* found missing, people start searching for her**: It was 7:30 a.m. Generally on such occasions, *Muthhachhi*, soon after her early morning *snaanam* (bath), would be the most active member, busy supervising, adding finishing touches and speaking sporadically and incessantly to one and all. It was unusual that she was not there in the scenario, right from the morning. People of the house had just then noticed her absence. Each one of the family started calling out her name, such that she would respond.

She was not in her room, her bed was properly made. This indicated that she had woken up. *Raghavan Chaeta* searched for her in all the places in the backyard including the cowshed and the steps leading to the pond and around. *Indu* searched for her in all the rooms downstairs, the portico. She asked *Beena chaechi* to go upstairs and find for her although there was a least possibility that she could have climbed the stairway to the top floor. *Beena chaechi* went to the garden and other places around the *tharavadu*. Calls for *Muttacchi* in different pitches by people of the house echoed in and around the *tharavadu*.

Father and son were puzzled at this development. Where could she have gone? *Beena chaechi* who had visited the washroom announced that *Mutthacchi* had had her bath as the clothes that she had discarded were soaked in soap water in the bucket.

*Radhakrishnan* put on his shirt and his slippers and stepped out of the portico announcing that he was going to find for his mother in the temple. He walked hurriedly on the mud road leading to the temple enquiring people he met on the way, whether they had seen his mothernearby. People replied that they had not noticed her. As *Radhakrishnan* reached the temple, he went around the main temple, met the 80 year old*pujari* / priest who was at the sanctum sanctorum.

The temple priest confirmed that *Asha chaechi* had come to the temple at 6:00 a.m. She was one among the few who had watched the morning *deepaaradhana* wherein, numerous lamps are lit and offered to the deity. He added that he distinctly recalled that she had received the sandalwood paste, vermillion and flowers in a plantain leaf as *prasadam* as distributed by him to the devotees. After that she moved on to perform the ritual of circumambulation of the temple *prakaaram* (outer part of the temple sanctum sanctorum).

*Radhakrishnan* went in search for his mother all around the temple premises. The temple *dharmakartaa* (superintendent) also joined him. The temple had a vast acreage of land with greenery all around. A small road led to the tank. Devotees would descend the steps on all the four sides of the tank to have a holy dip in the waters of the tank.

There were trees all around the tank and benches under the trees at intervals. From a distance, *Radhakrishnan* spotted his mother seated on a bench at one corner of the tank, under a *neem* tree. He was relieved to have spotted her. He ran to her. To his dismay, she sat motionless, with the folded plantain leaf containing the temple *prasaadam* in her hands. He shook her, by holding her shoulders and lo her head drooped on to a side. The temple *dharmakarta* held his fingers against her nostrils to check for her breath.

Sensing something wrong, a few people who were on the steps of the tank moved to the corner where *Radhakrishnan* and the temple *dharmakarta* were struggling with *Ashalata Menon* to help her regain senses. One of them sprinkled water on her face. A few of them called aloud, "*Amma! Amma...... Ammae.....!*"

However, all the efforts were in vain. Understanding the gravity of the situation, *Ganeshan* an acquaintance of *Radhakrishnan*, who happened to be there, tapped his shoulder and said that he had come by his car. He said, "*Let's not waste time! Let's carry Amma to the hospital, soon!*"

He added, *"There's a gate at the rear end of this temple tank which is a shorter way from here. I shall bring my car to that gate. Carry Amma to the gate! We shall shift her to the car and take her to the village hospital"*. Thus, eight people managed to carry *Amma* to the temple tank gate that was located a few yards away. It was a shorter way as well. *Radhakrishnan* was very disturbed, anxious and apprehensive. However, amidst this commotion, he had the sense to ask the *dharmakarta* to send information to his father. He also passed on to the *dharmakarta*, the telephone number of his youngest son *Vinod* at

*Trivandrum*. He requested the *dharmakarta* to ring up from his office, his son, asking him to come down to the village at the earliest.

Thus, *Ganeshan* drove his spacious Ambassador car, with *Ashalata Menon* lying in the rear seat with her head on *Radhakrishnan's* lap. He was silent and did not utter a word on the way to the village hospital. The 30 bedded village-hospital was developed by *Major Mahadevan*, a doctor, a native of the village, who had retired from the Army Hospital at *Lucknow*.

**News of *Ashalata Menon's* death dampens the spirit for *Vishukkani* celebrations:** At 9:30 a.m. *Ashalata Menon* was wheeled into the Emergency. Doctor *Major Mahadevan* examined her and checked her vitals. He could not feel her pulse. He asked the accompanying doctors to administer CPR (cardio pulmonary resuscitation) followed by defibrillation. He observed carefully the doctors in the process. None of these efforts could help *Ashalata Menon* revive her lost heart beats. Doctor *Major Mahadevan* walked out of the room and declared that the patient who was wheeled in was brought to the hospital dead. He added that she had breathed her last about an hour and half back. A lull of silence prevailed.

On learning that *Achhamma* had breathed her last; *Radhakrishnan* moved to the corner of the corridor and sat down on the wooden bench. He closed his eyes and took a deep breath. He prayed for her soul to attain salvation. *Radhakrishnan* could not contain himself. Tears continued to flow spontaneously. He found himself weak and weary.

*Ganeshan*, who was with the doctor, went into the emergency room, watched *Radhakrishnan Menon's* mother's face that had a serene expression, as she lay dead on the hospital bed. He touched her feet, as a mark of his homage and tributes to the departed soul.

## चलती चक्की देखकर दिया कबीरा रोए I
## दो पाटनके बीच में सबूत बचा ना कोई II

**Chalti Chakki dekh kar, diya Kabeera roye;**
**Do paatanke beech mein saboot bachaa na koi.**

*(Chalti Chakki)* The traditional manually driven grindstone; *(dekh kar)* on looking at; *(diya Kabeera roye)* Kabeer starts crying; *(Do)* Two; *(paatan)* a pair of round stones one above the other; *(ke beech)* caught in between; *(saboot bachaa na koi)* no grain remains gross/complete.

In this couplet by *Sant Kabir*h refers to death in the life of human beings as a grind. Therefore he cries at the sight of a traditional manual grindstone (made up of two circular stones, wherein the upper stone is rotated on the still lower stone) in action and says that as whole grains cannot remain whole when caught between the upper stone and the lower stone. Such is the 'grind of life'. No mortal being can escape death.

**<u>Radhakrishnan musters all his courage and springs to action:</u>** *Nandakishore* and *Ashalata's* son, gradually gained his composure, washed his face and moved to the room wherein his mother lay. He offered his last *pranaamam* to his mother's mortal body and her departed soul.

He visited an STD booth nearby and rang up his elder son *Manoj* followed by his younger son *Vinod* to break open the news about the death of their *Achhamma*. He asked them to inform his sons'-in-law *Santosh* and *Kartik-Vijay* about the demise of his mother such that they could accompany *Bindu* and *Sindhu* for the funeral.

He then rang up his father *Nandakishore Menon* to break open the news and informed that he would be arriving in an hour's time with his mother's 'body'. He had a word with *Raghavan Chaeta* and *Indu*, asking them to consult his father to make all arrangements, necessary for the funeral. With the help of *Ganeshan* he completed all the formalities and paperwork to claim the dead body, arrange for a van to transport the mortal remains of his mother to his ancestral home. *Nandakishore Menon* was unprepared for this development and thereby could not accept the news of the death of his wife and was quite disturbed and restless. Further, he had many questions that remained unanswered. A few of these questions were as follows: *Was Ashalata unwell? On this auspicious day of Vishu, why did she not come down to the Pooja room soon after her bath? Why did she choose to visit the temple without informing any one at home? Did she have a premonition of her death?*

However, he was alert enough to make a list of all the things that would be essential for the funeral. He contacted the priest to find out the right moment for the funeral. It was decided that the funeral would be held late afternoon, in the land behind the ancestral residence.

*Raghavan Chaeta* arranged for the erection a *pandal* in front of the porch. He also arranged for chairs and then he went in to procure the list of items, as prepared by *Nandakishore Menon* and essential for the funeral.

**Kith and kin assemble on the death of their near and dear ones:** Neighbours started thronging. The men-folk expressed their condolences to *NandakishoreMenon*, while the females went in to console the daughter-in-law, *Indu*. The van carrying the body of *Ashalata Menon* from the village hospital, entered in at about 11:30 a.m. People drew out the stretcher with the body from the van. *Nandakishore* had demarcated an area in the portico. The body clad in white with a small portion of the face visible, was rested on a longitudinally placed banana leaf on a raised plank, with the head kept towards the north. A burning oil lamp and incinerated incense sticks were kept near the head.

Family, friends and neighbours offered their obeisance to the departed soul. *Vinod* and *Sarita* arrived with their children at around 1:30 p.m. coincidentally *Manoj* was in *Bangalore* for an official trip. He sought permission for leave from his headquarters at Delhi and took a flight from *Bangalore* to *Kovalam*. He rang up his wife and broke the news. He asked her to reach *Kallada* by the earliest available bus. *Manoj* reached home by 2:00 p.m. followed by his wife Lavanya and children. *Santosh* along with his wife, *Bindu* and children had moved by then to *Thrissur* from *Chennai* to celebrate *Vishu* with his parents; thereby he co-ordinated with *Kartik-Vijay* and *Sindhu*. Thus all the eight of them, hired a SUV and reached the village by 2:30p.m.The atmosphere was charged with emotions off all kinds. The children recalled that *Muthhacchi* would always be there to receive them; however she was now lying supine on the bier ready to be consigned to flames. This was probably the first time that they were seeing a family member so close as a dead body.

**Cremation by sunset:** By 4:30 p.m. the *purohitan* (priest) started performing certain rites. The female members watched all the proceedings from a distance. All the male members of the family i.e. *Nandakishore, Radhakrishnan, Raghavan Chaetan, Manoj, Vinod, Santosh, Kartik-Vijay,Vipin, Kartik- Vignesh, Nandu* and other menfolk all being barefooted and bare bodied with just a white *veshti* / loin-cloth and *angavastram* around their shoulders carried the body on the bier to the cremation spot to place on the pyre that was made ready. After a few rituals as guided by the *purohitar*; *Nandakishore* and *Radhakrishnan* lit the funeral pyre made of sandal-wood logs and dung cakes. It was dusk. All waited patiently and silently until the body was consigned to the flames. The process is referred to as '*dahanam*'. *Manoj* and *Vinod* consoled *Nandu* and *Kartik-Vignesh* as they could not bear the sight of their beloved great-grandmother burning.

*Nandakishore* and *Radhakrishnan* recalled all the happenings from dawn to dusk. And now, on this day the body of *Ashalatha Menon* who lived on this planet for 85 years had merged into the *Panchatatwa* or the five elements of nature viz. earth, air, water, fire / sun and the ether / sky.

All the male members had their bath in the pond in the backyard. The females washed the house and had their bath in the washroom. All were tired and exhausted with the turn of affairs with the death of *Mutthacchi*. All felt that *Muttachhi* had probably negotiated with *kaalan / yama*, the death God that she should be taken away from this planet on the auspicious day of *Vishu*; leaving the family members bereaved. The cows in the cow-shed could also sense the melancholy in the air and they started bellowing unusually. *Radhakrishnan* and *Raghavan Chaeta* had to pacify them.

**Family members gather and mourn over *Mutthachhi's* demise after the funeral:** As guided by customs and rituals, there had to be no cooking at home on this day of cremation and two days to follow. Thereby, friends and neighbours pooled in to provide the family with meals for the three days. All the family members sat cross-legged on the floor in a circle. *Indu* and *Beena Chaechhi* served the meal provided by the neighbours on plates made by stitched leaves. All, except the children had no appetite or desire to consume anything as all were entangled in thoughts related to *Muttacchhi*.

*Muttacchan* broke his ruling of not engaging oneself in conversation during meals. As he had his first morsel, he asked *Manoj* and *Vinod* as well as *Bindu* and *Sindhu* whether they had had any kind of communication or conversation over the telephone with *Ashalata* in the past week. All of them replied in affirmative. They said in chorus that on 10<sup>th</sup> April, *Muttachhi* had greeted all the four of them and their family members, for the ensuing *Vishu* celebrations. *Manoj* said that she was specifically annoyed with him when he mentioned that he would not be with his family on *Vishu* on account of his official trip to Bangalore. She had specifically asked all the four of them to ensure that all of them planned at least a three-week stay together along with their children, at *Kallada*, during the forthcoming vacation. This was when she spoke to them about the locksmith *Rashid* from *Kovalam* and his commitment to make the keys to the two chests with her age-old belongings. She had also mentioned that this time the children would be happy and she would also be happy to display all her possessions to them.

*Nandakishore Menon* sighed deeply and got up after he was through supper. He paced thoughtfully for quite some time in the portico. *Radhakrishnan* asked his wife *Indu* to be alert and observant such that his father was never left out alone, for it was a difficult time ahead for him to cope up with, without his consort. Meanwhile, *Bindu* and *Sindhu* made arrangements for all to sleep on grass / *korai* mats that were laid symmetrically on the floor, as sleeping on beds and mattresses had to be avoided till the rituals that would last tillfifteen days of mourning.

Before going to sleep, the two sons and sons'-in-law had a conversation with their grandfather and parents, in order to find out about the course of proceedings for further fifteen days. *Nandakishore Menon*, explained to his sons and grandsons that the 16 day mourning period was traditionally followed by the *Menons'* and *Nairs'* as per the *sanatana-dharma* (Hindu philosophy) *antimasamskara* (final rites after death). It is believed that *dahanam* (cremation) helps in the salvation of the *sthoola deha* (physical body); whereas the *sookshma aatma* (abstract/micro form of soul) that leaves the body soon after (*mrityu*) traverses beyond the planet, across different realms of energy levels to attain *moksha / mukti* (salvation).

Thereby, after *asthi-sanchayanam* (the collection of the bones of the body) from the pyre and dissolution of the bones into the waters of flowing water/rivers, on the third day of *dahanam*; daily *tharpanam* (offerings to the departed soul) is regularly done by the *kartaa* (the person who lights the pyre and performs the rituals) to facilitate the soul detach from worldly-ties and transcend step by step to the final realm of salvation.

*Nandakishore* was quite a practical person. He could very well understand the limitations of his grandsons and granddaughters as well as granddaughters'-in-law and grand sons'-in-law as salaried employees for a prolonged stay for the rituals.

Similarly the children's new session had just begun and they had to rush to school. He was grateful to each one of them for having come down with their children at such a short notice, to be present for the last rites of his wife at her funeral. Thereby he said that it was essential that they stay till the third day. They could then rejoin on the tenth day or the thirteenth day for the final rites.

Observing all the happenings around, the seven children had a number of questions bothering them. A few of their questions were as follows: *Why do people die? Why cannot we know about the exact time and date of death? If our souls move away after death, why can't we see our souls or others souls while we are living? Why are there so many rituals? Who designed these rituals and traditions? Do souls visit the planet once they attain 'moksha'? etcetra, etcetra, etcetra.*

Their *acchan* and *amma* did not have the time or patience to answer all their questions. When they would not have the right answers or explanations, they would either ask them to stay put or shoo them away to their *muthhachhan* or their grandparents.

Amidst all this chaos, the children spotted late *Muttacchi's* pair of locked chests in her room. They grew glum. Their enthusiasm to unlock the treasures had dwindled. They had tears in their eyes and wished that it would have been such a happy moment, if and only if their great-grandmother would herself have had unlocked the chests and displayed all her belongings.

*Bindu* and *Sindhu* decided to stay back at the village, after having spoken to their respective employers, and getting their leave sanctioned. Since their children had a few days of school before the vacation. They were sent away along with their father *Santosh* and *Kartik-Vijay*. *Manoj* proceeded to *Delhi*. *Lavanya*, *Vipin*, and *Shailaja* proceeded along with *Vinod*, *Sarita*, *Mythili* and *Nandu* to *Trivandrum*. *Vinod* had planned that after leaving his wife, children, *Manoj's* wife and children at their respective destination he would daily commute to his office from his village, till all the rituals were over.

### Part 4

**'Shuddhi karanam'// Sanctification**: All rituals were over. It was 29th April of the year, the sixteenth day also known as *shodasham*, after the death of *Muttachhi*, *Shrimati Ashalata Menon*, great-grandmother of *Saptaswarangal*. Once again all the sixteen family members assembled on the occasion, prayers were offered, and the lamp in the prayer room of the family was lit with the commencement of *'nityapooja'*. This day also marked the final day of *'moksha'* / salvation attained by the departed soul. Thus this day marked a day of transition from mourning to normal lifestyle. All the family members visited the temple together as a token of acknowledging the same.

As they stepped into the temple, *Radhakrishnan* could not help recalling the tragic day of *Vishu* and this place where his mother had breathed her last. He had to console himself. The temple priest was in the sanctum sanctorum decorating the deity and offering the deity *archana* and chanting the *ashtotramantra*. As he came out to distribute *prasaadam* to the devotees, he paused and took time in speaking to *Nandakishore Menon* and *Radhakrishnan Menon*. He said, *"Tragic incidents are momentary, life goes on, continue to do little things and good deeds daily, and find happiness and solace."*

**_Mutthacchhan_ finally unlocks _Ashalata Menon's_ chests of treasures**: The entire family walked back to return home after the temple visit. On their way back,

*Mutthacchan* announced addressing the children, "*Makkale! / Children! This evening, you shall have your most cherished desire fulfilled!*"

*Nandu* and *Kartik-Vignesh* asked curiously, "*Is it an ice-cream party muttaccha?*"

"*No!*" replied *muttacchan* and added, "*You have two more chances to guess*".

*Rituja, Shailaja* and *Jalaja* said in a chorus, "*Do we have an instrumental music concert, this evening? Muttacchan* turned his head from left to right to indicate that they were wrong.

*Vipin* and *Mythili* exclaimed, "*Then it must be 'theyyam' performance by Girishankar Nair and party.*"

"*No one is correct! Wait and watch!All of you are required to assemble at home at 6:30 p.m. in the central hall downstairs!*"

**A long wait for the surprise:** The seven cousins assembled in the central hall at 6:00p.m. They were impatient and keen to soon discover what the surprise was? The elders in the family took *Mutthacchan* casually. They thought that *Nandakishore Menon* wanted to amuse the children in some way. However they walked in one by one and accommodated themselves by 6:25 p.m. *Muttacchan* walked in waving his wooden walking stick. His moustache with pointed ends directed upwards gave him an authoritative look. As soon as he entered the hall, looking atall the family members present in the hall, he chuckled and said, "*Aha!*" He checked and confirmed whether everyone was present.

He called for *Radhakrishna* and *Raghavan* and told them something in their ears and signalled them to bring in whatever it was! Both of them walked out of the hall towards *Muttachhi's* room. Each one of them came dragging two huge box-like structures on rollers. Each one of them was covered on all sides with a red velvet cover with golden motifs. They were placed at the centre of the hall. *Vipin* and *Mythili* cried together and exclaimed, *"They are Muttacchi's chests, great-grandma's chest of treasures!"*

*"Marvellous!"* shouted *Muttachhan*, *"I thought that you would have easily made what the surprise, yesterday when I talked about the surprise!" Saptaswarangal* said in chorus, *"At last we shall get to know what Muttachhi has stored in these two chests!"*

"Yes *makkale*, as soon as we contacted *Rashid*, the locksmith, in the first week of April, your *Muttachhi* was keen on displaying all her possessions to you all, this vacation". She told me, *"We should not waste further time; the children were quite disappointed during their visit in Christmas break just because we had lost the keys. They should not be disappointed, this vacation"*

*"All these days as I was mourning, I was quite troubled that she chose to leave me alone, although we had promised each other that we would be partners for this lifetime!" Muttacchan* said. *"For the past few days, as I would walk into her room, these two chests that were brought into her room on 13$^{th}$ April kept haunting me. Thereby I decided why wait for the vacation? Why do we not avail this opportunity when all children would be there for the sixteenth day of shubham!"*

He ceremoniously, unveiled both the chests and fondly ran his fingers on the labels on both the chests inscribed with *Muthhachhi's* name. Meanwhile *Raghavan* unlocked both the chests and raised the lid of the first one. The metallic hinges of the lid made a creaking sound, till it stood at a right-angle to the chest container. A white satin cloth covered the items below. *Radhakrishnan* removed the muslin cloth and took out the following things from **Chest No. 1**

- A red cloth bag full of nickel coins with King George's head (of different denominations)
- Five green bags each filled with a variety of *kaudi/ kowri /* seashells.
- A mirror with an ornamentally designed sandalwood frame.
- A set of five combs made of sandal wood.
- An ornamentally designed cylindrical box with about a hundred miniature animal figures in ivory.
- A pair of Japanese hand fans.
- A velvet cloth bag full of pebbles, each pebble had a face painted on.
- Twenty large Conch shells of different kinds.
- Two pairs of *Chilanga / Ghungroo/* Ankletbells.
- Zenith Company Brass antique pocket watch in a wooden box.
- A pair of mariner's compass in a wooden box.

- 50 Miniature brass idols of animals and deities.
- A miniature globe, a medium sized globe and a large globe
- Black and white photographs of *AshalataMenon's* parents, *NandakishoreMenon's* photograph in his army uniform.
- A small photo album with black and white pictures of *AshalataMenon*, across different ages.
- A brass bust of the Trinity (*Brahma, Vishnu, Maheshwara*)

The children were amused with *Muttachhi's* collection in Chest No. 1. They were also disappointed as they had expected lots of gold, gemstones and valuable jewellery as they had seen in chests looted by pirates in comics and films. *Vipin* was surprised to find that all the articles were well preserved and packed. *Radhakrishnan Menon* elaborated that the yester-year preservatives in vogue were well dried tobacco leaves, *neem* leaves, pepper and spices.

*Muttachhan* directed *Raghavan* to get the next Chest opened. The lid of this chest was much heavier than the lid of the former chest; although both appeared to be a replica of the same. A purple satin cloth was spread to cover the items below. When *Raghavan* removed the cloth he found that there were many more articles in this chest. Here is a list of the things found in the **Chest No. 2**:

- A white large brocaded sling bag with a dozen of 9 inches long chains made up of pearls.

- In a similar large brocaded pink bag were yet another dozen of shorter chains, a pair each of amethyst, emerald, and garnet, jade, ruby and sapphire gemstones.

- A jewellery box with a set of ornaments made up of beautifully designed corals viz. a necklace, two pairs of bangles, a pair of eartops, a broad bracelet, an amulet and a waist band.

- A designer cardboard box with a set of cut silverware viz. two pairs of glasses, bowls, spoons, tray and a jug like teapot and milk-pot.

- An intricately designed (filigree) temple complex made of silver.

- A beautifully designed filigree chariot depicting *Parthasarathy* (Lord Krishna) as the charioteer and *Arjuna*.

- In a leather folder there were about more than 60 paintings, each one (A4 sized unframed canvas) with the signature of *Ashalata*. (Children greatly admired these paintings. *Bindu*, *Sindhu*, *Vinod* and *Manoj* had never known about this admirable talent of *Acchamma*. On seeing these paintings, *Muthhacchan* further explained that she was passionate about painting before her marriage, however she gradually lost touch with painting)

- In a large canvas bag were a dozen dolls, each with beautiful hair and face. Each one of them was in different costumes and had varied skin colour;

representing the following nationalities: Africa, Australia, China, Japan, India, Turkey, Russia, Spain, Netherlands, Scotland, Germany and Korea.

➢ Tied up in a cloth bundle were a few framed photographs. On untying the bundle the following were seen captured in black and white Kodak photographs:

i. a vintage model car that *Muttachhan* had bought when he was 28 years old,

ii. *Ashalata Menon's* parents and *Nandakishore's* parents,

iii. *Ashalata Menon* with her elder brothers and a younger sister,

iv. *Ashalata* and *Nandakishore* with the parents of both of them during their wedding,

v. Wedding day photograph of *Muthhachhi* and *Mutthacchan*.

➢ There was a box with lots of wooden toys some were bright and colourful and some were brownin colour.

➢ Another small box had miniature models of musical instruments viz. *ektaara, veena, mridangam, manjira, trumpet, table and dhagga, chhenduvaadyam* (temple drums of Kerala), violin, accordion and harmonium.

**Waves of nostalgia:** When the first chest was opened, children had lots of expectations and there was a lot of noise and clamour; as some exclaimed, a few sighed. There were cries of bewilderment and amusement as well. Initially, it was the curiosity of the cousins; but as the chests were opened and the treasures were displayed, the adults also got involved and were deeply immersed in viewing the collection.

*Manoj* was reminded of the *SalarJung* museum that he had visited in *Hyderabad*, long....long ago! He commented that all the articles could be kept in a museum rather than being locked in a chest. *Manoj, Vinod, Bindu* and *Sindu* had never earlier seen the snapshots of their great-grandparents which they could see this day!

*Radhakrishnan* and his father felt relieved that they could keep up *Ashalata's* promise to the children; howeverit would have been so good if *Ashalata* would have been present to enjoy these moments with the entire family!

To conclude this story here is a quote: *"Providence has its appointed hour for everything. We cannot command results, we can only strive."*

Mahatma Gandhi

\*\*\*\*\*\*\*\*\*\*\*\*\*\*\*\*\*\*\*\*\*\*\*\*\*\*\*\*\*\*\*\*\*\*\*\*\*\*

# The Death of a Primate

**What are primates?** Around 65 million years ago, during the Palaeocene epoch, shortly after the mass extinction of the dinosaurs, there appeared a small nocturnal primate named *Omomyx* in the North American continent. The word primate is derived from a Latin word *primas* meaning the 'forerunner' or 'the first' or 'the chief.' In 1758, taxonomist, *Carolos Von Linnaeus*, first used this term for the highest order of mammals. They were regarded as the most advanced and closest to human beings. Human beings are the most evolved among the primates. The group includes a range of mammals that include **lemurs, lorises, tarsiers, monkeys and apes;** all united by their shared characteristics and evolutionary history. Following are the characteristics of primates' viz.

➢ Large brain-to-body mass ratio indicating cognitive abilities;

➢ Binocular and stereoscopic vision, owing to their forward facing eyes that enable the perception of one image and the depth of the object.

➢ Flexible limbs (hands and feet). The Simian line in the palms that accounts for opposable thumb; this feature helps primates to grasp, hold, climb and manipulate objects. The plantigrade, feet (walking on the soles) are also well adapted to withstand the weight of the body, jump, climb and run.

- The peak of evolution is acquiring the 'upright posture', thus helping them to walk on two legs also referred to as being bipedal. This allows the usage of hands for many other purposes.
- Claws on the digits of mammals are modified to flat nails in case of primates.
- Adapted to consume omnivorous diet cooked food, grains, pulses, vegetables, fruits, insects, raw / cooked meat and flesh.
- Long gestation periods and slow maturation
- All primates are bestowed with the voice to communicate. Vocal expressions, facial expressions and body language are used to express emotions and convey information.
- Primates exhibit kinship or social behaviour. They generally live in large groups, they are gregarious and have a complex organisational structure and order; with an effective communication system.

**Backdrop of this story:** This story about this *vaanara* / monkey is an outcome of a real life observation of an incident during my tenure as a School Principal at an industrial township named *Grasim Vihar* in a village named *Rawan* situated in the *Tehsil* of *Simga* of district of *Balodabazar*, currently in the State of *Chhattisgarh*. It was in the year 2000, on November 1, that *Chattisgarh* attained statehood being carved out from the state of *MadhyaPradesh*. This belt of *Chhattisgarh* has numerous Cement factories as the area is rich in limestone, the chief ingredient of Cement. The township is accessible by road from *Raipur*, the capital city of *Chhattisgarh*; from *Bhatapara*, a commercial town located on the Howrah-Mumbai railway line; as well as from district *Balodabazar*and cities like *Bilaspur* and *Raigarh.*

I had first visited this Cement Township named *Grasim Vihar* in the month of April, in the year, 1997. I started from *Bhilai*, a steel township and reached the cement township via Raipur, in about three hours' time. Although I had earlier quite often heard about *Balodabazar* and *Bhatapara*; courtesy a programme titled 'Listener's Choice of Film Songs' broadcasted by Radio Ceylon / Sri Lanka. I would be amused as there were quite a few names of listeners' requests for their choice of *Bollywood* songs from places viz. *Jhumri Talayya*, *Naya Jalna*, *Balodabazar* and *Bhatapara*. This also kindled in me the curiosity to know more about these places as well as the listeners' who were named often.

Later, I came to know that *Jhumri Talayya* was located in *Jharkhand* (w.e.f. 15/11/2000) formerly a part of *Bihar*; *Naya Jalna* in Maharashtra and *Balaodabazar* and *Bhatapara* in *Chhattisgarh* (a part of *Madhya Pradesh* till 31st October 2000).

**Varying contours and scenario, as I travelled across the suburbs of Raipur:** I was familiar with the contours of *Bhilai* and *Raipur*. The macadamised road was not so broad, although there were quite many heavy vehicles (trucks & payload carriers) along with different brands of cars, vans and jeeps moving on the road. On either side of the road were full grown trees of different species viz. Sal (*Shorea robusta*), Arjun (*Terminalia arjuna*), Mahua (*Madhuca longifolia*), Gulmohar (*Delonix regia*), Banyan (*Ficus benghalensis*), Pipal (*Ficus religiosa*), Palash (*Butea monosperma*), Gular (*Ficus racemosa*), Neem (*Azadirachta indica*), Kadamba (*Neolamarckia cadamba*), Indian plum (*Zizyphus jujuba*) and many more. At a few points, I could spot a few monkeys with their brood, on trees as well as on the roadside.

At the initial stretch of about 10 Kilometres, I could spot farms on either side. This was when I first noticed an *Emu* farm / ranch. I could see a pair of *Emu* birds strutting in the farm. I was surprised to see birds that were native to Australia living in the plains of India. I was tempted to get down and observe, interact and enquire about the birds in the farm. However, my mission was to reach *Grasim Vihar*, well before lunch such that I would have a fair idea about the locality and the school that I was expected to join by May, 1997.

I noticed through the window of the vehicle that I was travelling by; that despite the heat of the month, there was a lot of movement and hustle-bustle in the surroundings. I passed through a few villages, meadows, canals; small *dhaabas* (eating courts / tea and food vending stalls) on the roadside. At many stretches the roads were quite bumpy with potholes. Half-way through the path to *Grasim Vihar*, the driver crossed a school; he stopped the vehicle, in the village market square, near a tea-shop. I was told that this is a village named *Kharora*. I could see a line of trucks, jeeps and cars on the left side of the road. There were quite a few shops each one thronged by drivers of different vehicles and quite a few passengers. The drivers had taken a break from their long hours of driving to refresh themselves with a hot drink and obviously it was tea. The vehicle driver asked me, if I would have tea? I refused, as it was too hot. A few other passengers also had tea with snacks viz. the popular *samosa*, *poha* and *jalebi*, potato *chops*.

The market place of *Kharora* was quite crowded. There were lot many shops viz. fruit mart, vegetable mart, sweet shop a shop catering to the sale of vessels and utensils, cloth shop, a small jewellery shop, shops catering to framing of pictures and photographs, shops with pots and pitchers and many more. Cows and buffaloes walked past the road.

The driver returned after 15 minutes and drove ahead on the same road. The road was quite bad; however the driver manoeuvred the vehicle skilfully, so did the other vehicle and truck drivers.We crossed a few more villages which had small, medium and large houses. I could spot black boars and pigs moving in groups. They grunted as they moved from the roadside into the fields. A few fields had tractors and water pumps for irrigation. The small and medium houses were made up of clay with thatched roofs. The walls of the houses and the front yard were mopped clean with wet mud and dung. The walls had hand paintings in red. These paintings were similar to *Worli* paintings, depicting trees and village folk engaged in differentjobs viz. pounding and winnowing rice, harvesting as well as dancing in rows and circles. Children played under the tree-shade. Cocks and hens with their brood of chicks were also found pecking at grains in the yard. The large houses were *pucca* houses made up of concrete and were well distempered.

At a distance in the horizon, the chimneys of the cement silos were visible, indicating that we would be soon approaching village named *Hirmi*, which then had the Larsen and Toubro Unit of Cement factory abbreviated as the L&T Cement Company. As the car passed this factory's railway siding track and truck yard; the driver announced that our destination was 12 Kms. ahead. The flora and fauna was almost the same throughout the way. Further, half way through, we crossed the area named *Jhipan*, which had the open limestone mines. Open spaces and areas showed the presence of red and yellow alluvial soil. After a 15 minute drive, as we approached the T- junction of village *Rawan*, we could spot the entire cement plant, at a distance. Display boards on the way indicated the way to Grasim Cement Works at *Rawan*.Ultimately, at 11:00 a.m. we reached the gate of the township named *GrasimVihar*. Thus I stepped into an abode where I happemed to live for more than sixteen years. I have presented a detailed account of this place as well as the School where I worked, in my first book titled, "Golden Summers". In this Chapter of my second book; I shall now present the story about the primate that appears in the title of this Chapter.

**Monkeys at *Grasim Vihar* Township:** Who is not attracted to or amused by a monkey? Almost all; be it a child or an adult. As I settled at the township, functioning as the Principal of the school, I gradually got to know about the surroundings. Whenever I would hear crows cawing in a group, it indicated either that they had either spotted a snake, or a cat or a group of monkeys. It was a cautionary / alert call.

Rhesus monkeys (*Macaca mulatta*) and grey *langurs* (*Semnopithecus entellus*) were regular visitors from nearby forests and villages. They always visited in groups. Purpose of visit was in search of food and water. Monkeys are generally frugivorous (fruit eating); although some eat leaves, flowers, tubers and a few feedon insects and small animals. They were well adapted to their arboreal mode of life especially in climbing trees and heights and leaping from one point to the other.

**Pranks played by the gang of monkeys:** I lived in one of the four quarters in the ground floor residence of a two storey building.There was a doorway with an iron grill door that opened into the terraces above both the quarters of the first floor. We would get to know the arrival of the gang monkeys, with the noise that was generated by them as each one of them enjoyed jumping from the grill door to the terrace parapet. The grill door would slide back to the wooden frame of the door with a bang. This would recur with each member of the entire troupe repeating the same act. Many a time, while in my garden, when I would gaze upward, I would find the tail of the monkey dangling down from the roof parapet of the terrace above the first floor. The dangling tail looked exactly like a rope / snake. In my garden there was a mango tree. One summer, it was for the first time that I saw the tree laden with fruits. One afternoon a group of monkeys visited the tree and had a good feast of them, disappointing me and my family members who were eagerly waiting to taste the fruits once the fruits would ripen.

The group always had a leader or two (males) with many followers of different sizes. The little ones generally clung on to the bellies of their mothers. It was interesting to watch them jump and glide from one tree to the other, or one roof of a building to the other. The females also were often found grooming the males and the little ones by nit picking as they dexterously separated the hairs of the scalp / skin to locate for a louse or the nits that were clinging to the hairs of the primate.

We had to be very careful at school, as children were very fond of watching the activities and pranks played by the monkeys that would also be found on the trees surrounding the school premises. If the time of thevisit by the gang of monkeys coincided with the school recess, we had to be further cautious to avoid mishaps with the possibility of the monkeys snatching the food that the children had in their open lunch boxes / snack boxes / hands. We had to warn children to be cautious and be aware of the consequences of being scratched by the nails of the monkey or its teeth bite.

I had often heard of and read in newspapers that during summers when the sun scorched and the temperatures soared high, water reservoirs, ponds, lakes, tanks and wells would dry up. Gangs of monkeys visiting human settlement areas and villages would jump into dried wells that were quite deep, ending up their lives. Many wondered if this was a deliberate 'mass suicide' or an accidental happening.

**The day's incident:** It was around 1:30 p.m. in the afternoon hours of a week day in the second week of May, 1999. Although it was vacation time for the entire school, the school Office, Computer Department and Library were functioning for interested students. It was time to go home for lunch. I took my bag and walked to the long stretch of parking area, adjacent to the compound wall, demarcated for parking cycles, motor cycles, scooters and cars. I walked to my car that was parked in a take-off mode such that I could easily steer the vehicle and move towards the gate that was on the left. As I was unlocking the car door, I spotted a well built grey *langur* sitting in a meditative posture on the floor of the empty parking slot to the left of my car. The tall primate with a black face and head with a bushy mane, was sitting with its back resting along the compound wall, with hands on its thighs and legs outstretched. I started the car, curious to watch the reaction of the primate. The animal, did not move although it opened its eyes, as I steered out the vehicle to the gate. Opposite to this gate, across the road was a small Shiva Temple. At the gate I moved to the right and after a short length of drive I reached home. I washed my face and hands and sat down to have my lunch. After attending to odd jobs in the kitchen, removing all the clothes on the clothesline that had dried up, folding each one of them well and stacking them up in the cupboard, I watched the news being aired on the TV. Soon after a short nap, I realised that it was 2:45 p.m. and it was time to go back to my office at School.

**The development:** As I parked my vehicle in the allotted space in the same parking area, I was surprised to see the primate in the same position as I had seen it at half past one. It was three in the afternoon and I wondered whether it was natural for a primate to be in this posture for such a long time. I tried making some noise to distract the animal; however it continued to remain in the same meditative posture, and did not open its eyes, this time. The posture adopted by this primate, now reminded me of *Ramabhakta Hanuman*, the *brahmachari* (celibate) monkey, venerated and worshipped by majority of the *Hindus*.

After locking my car, I walked into the school in a pensive mood. The school peon accosted me and opened the door to my room. I told him about the solitary *langur* in the parking area, near the gate and expressed that there seemed to be something wrong with it as it appeared to be quite slack and tired, which is unlikely of a monkey / *langur*. The peon replied casually that it must be sitting there to escape heat. Meanwhile, the School Accountant who was there to submit the files with daily reports to me for verification and endorsement; had overheard my conversation with the peon. He signalled the peon to move along with him to the spot and assured me that he would look into the matter.

I got immersed in looking into the papers in the files, when the peon came in panting and informed me that the animal was probably dead. The Accountant and the peon had hurled twigs and small objects at the animal, however, to their surprise it did not react. The Accountant immediately rang up the Security Department of Grasim Cement Company, informing them about the situation and soliciting their assistance and intervention.

**Human intervention to rescue the primate**: It was 3:45 p.m. when the Security Officer, came in. He visited the spot and rang up his team to reach the school. According to him the animal was sick, and not dead. He came into my office and rang up his senior administrative officer, informing him about the development. The senior officer asked him to ensure two things in the operation **i.** Safety and Security, and **ii.** To ensure that the animal was in no way hurt as handling animals was a very sensitive issue, then.

I came out with the officer and reached the spot. Both of us were taken aback to see by then about 35 to 40 monkeys; a few on the gate doors, a few on the compound wall, a few of them at the temple gate and majority of them scattered on the trees near this parking area. Although it was 4 p.m. it was quite hot as temperatures ranged in thisplacefrom $35^0$C to $42^0$ C, during summers.

**Social behaviour displayed by the assembly of monkeys:** As 6 security guards entered the place with rods, planks and gunny bags, about 8 monkeys sat in a semicircle in front of the *langur*, guarding the animal as a defence mechanism. The animals on the gate started whooping, screeching and chattering; outwitting the security personnel. Meanwhile the ones on the compound wall started pacing the wall, as though they were on a protest march. We were taken for yet another surprise when each one of the monkey sitting in a semicircle bowed and touched the feet of the *langur*, one by one, as though they were offering their obeisance to the primate. This confirmed that the primate was dead, although it was still sitting upright, with its hind legs stretched straight. The remaining monkeys would not budge from their vantage points. Further they would not allow any human being to approach the resting primate.

**The rescue strategy:** The Security Officer, the supervisors and the security guards discussed to develop a strategy, to somehow or the other, shoo away the 40 monkeys, in order to reach the primate. Meanwhile the guards brought in a portable electronic siren, clang discs, crackers and explosives. The road to the temple was cordoned off. The monkeys guarding the primate in the parking area were startled by the noise of explosion of a series of crackers, followed by the bellowing electric siren. They started running helter-skelter. Those on the compound wall fled to the trees at a distance. The screeched, chattered and snarled at the people. Once the area was cleared off, the guards were quick enough to move to the primate with a stretcher. They were initially hesitant and shuddered to touch the animal. Their supervisor bellowed at them when they sprang into action. Two of them held the primate by its shoulders, while the other two held its legs and transferred the listless and motionless animal to the stretcher and covered it with gunny sacks. The stretcher was held by the same four guards; the primate was then shifted to a motorised cart vehicle that was used to carry cement bags from the packaging unit to the storage unit. By the time all this took place, it was 5:45 p.m. Since it was summer, dusk had not set in as yet.

**Reflections on the death of the primate:** As we were moving back, the peon said to me, "*Mam, it is Tuesday today, the day dedicated to the worship of Bajrangbali (Hanuman). Is it a good omen that the monkey had to die on this day at our school premises?*" I replied, "*May be, it found this place peaceful to attain moksha! Consider that the primate had come down to bless this institution on this day and chose to breathe his last!*" Meanwhile the School administrative officer asked for my car keys to park my vehicle out. The other staff members also parked their two wheelers out. He got the entire parking lot disinfected.

At 6:30 p.m. as I moved out to get into my car, I saw that the peon had lit an earthen lamp and had offered some flowers at the spot where the primate was found dead. That was his faith. I offered my mute salutation to the departed soul! On the way back home, I pondered on the following points; be it animals or human beings, death is inevitable. We rejoice at instances of birth, however cannot accept death at its face value. Kith and kin mourn at one's death, prolong this mourning for a period of time; however over a period of time; the individual is remembered on a few occasions or may gradually be forgotten. This is probably true for all primates.

Did the primate have a premonition about its death? Did it worry about the fate of its parents, spouse and children, while dying? Did it have an undisclosed wish or an unfulfilled desire, while dying? I am sure that the answers to all these questions would be a big NO! However my thought process was so because, despite being an evolved primate, my brain and thought process as a humanoid is programmed so, and conditioned in the same line as any other human being does! Unfortunately human beings love to multiply their worries and anxiety! Here is another couplet on fear of death by *Sant Kabir* :

**जिस मरनै थै जग डरै, सो मेरे आनंद।**
**कब मरि हूँ कब देखि हूँ, पूरन परमानंद।।**

*(Jiss marne hai)* The death that; *(Jag Darai)* the people of the world are afraid of; *(So mere Anand)* that death is the source of my happiness; *(Kab mari hoon?)* waiting for the moment when I shall die *(Kab dekhi hoon)* waiting for the moment when I shall see the Almighty; *(Pooran Paramanand)* I shall attain divine and eternal bliss.

Death, that the entire world is afraid of, I find happiness and bliss in that death. I keep waiting for the moment such that I shall discard my body on this earth, meet and see the Supreme Power / Almighty and achieve happiness of the Supreme order!

Thus the death of the primate was just not an event but a moment to introspect, respect our position as a member of the most evolved species, on this planet. Let's learn to live and honour our birth and existence on this planet as mortal beings!

*******************************

# SEASHELLS

# An Interlude to the Second Set of Stories

*"A beach is not only a sweep of sand, but shells of sea creature, the sea glass, the seaweed, the incongruous objects washed up by the ocean"– Henry Grunwald*

People lay on the sands of the beach, enjoying the breeze, the sunshine and the noise of the sea. Some gazed aimlessly at the horizon where they could spot one or two boats and ships on the move. Children and adults enjoyed the play of the turbulent tides that was almost clocked to strike the shore line and recede. The incoming tides brought to the shore slugs, crabs, star fishes, clams and many more shelled creatures. Quite a few people, who walked on the beach, spotted a number of seashells without the soft bodied mollusc within. They were amazed at the sight of multitude and variety of seashells. Grandparents who were accompanied by grandchildren to the beach; narrated legends and stories related to the vast sea, sea creatures, mystical mermaid and mermen. They also told them the key lessons that they could take from seashells, *"Life is a short but beautiful journey, and eternity depends on the legacy we leave behind. Shells also remind us to be strong and resilient with the right mindset to meet all the challenges and control all aspects of our lives."*

The two stories that follow this interlude are dedicated to the 'seashells' and the 'soft bodied creatures' that are equipped to create these shells. However here is a brief account on the study of sea-shells.

**Malacology & Conchology:** The study of the entire mollusc (soft bodied invertebrate) with its shell is known as *malacology*, whereas the study of the shells alone is termed as *conchology*. Molluscs are both freshwater and marine species, although the seashells found on the sea beaches are all generated by the marine species. The shells found on riverbanks are generally of those of the freshwater species. People who collect seashells are known as conchologists. There are about more than 100,000 species; thereby conchologists tend to specialize in their field of collection.

The soft body of the mollusc, such as snails, bivalves and chitons have a skin like tissue covering their body known as the mantle. It is this layer that secretes a substance chiefly composed of calcium carbonate and a protein named chitin. Seashells are usually made up of several layers of distinct microstructures that have differing mechanical properties. The shell layers are secreted by different parts of the mantle although incremental growth takes place only at the shell margin. Thusthe calcareous and chitin richseashellsare classified into the following:

> ➤ **Gastropods:** molluscs generally single shelled / univalve (apple snails, cowries, cones etc.)
> ➤ **Bivalvia:** molluscs that have a pair of symmetrical shells (clams, oysters and mussels)
> ➤ **Aplacophores:** molluscs without plates (cylindrical worm like sea cucumbers)

- **Monoplacophores:** molluscs with a single plate only one species found in Costa Rica.
- **Polyplacophores:** molluscs with at least eight plates for e.g. Chiton.
- **Scaphopods:** molluscs that are boat footed with tusk shaped cells for e.g, tuskshells
- **Cephalopods:** molluscs that are head footed with internal shells viz. Cuttle-fish and Octopus

<u>Commercial value of Shells</u>: Naturally available seashellsare collected from the coastline beaches of countries like the *Phillipines, Indonesia, India, Brazil, Mexico and the Carribbean*. In India, the seashell collection and marketing is popular in the beaches of *Kanyakumari, Gokarna, Kovalam, Puducherry, Mangalore, Kaup, Udupi, Malpe, Manipl, Varanga, Baindur, Eco Beach at Honnavar, Tadadi Port, Kumta, Puri, Konark, Digha, Mandarmani, Calangute, Anjuna, Mumbai, Ratnagiri, Ganpatipule, Kutch, Jamgar, Porbandar* and parts of *Lakshadweep and Andaman & Nicobar Islands*.

The shell trade supports local economies and provides income for coastal communities. However it is mandatory and essential to ensure sustainable and eco-friendly collection practices to protect marine ecosystems and preserve the resources of shell for the forthcoming generations. **The naturally available seashell collection and marketing industry** follow a process that involves:

- **Collection:** Shells are gathered from beaches, reefs and ocean floors either manually or by equipments like dredges and trawls. Collectors often target specific species or types of shells.

➤ **Cleaning and Sorting:** The seashells that are collected are cleaned well to remove the organisms or their debris, dirt and sand. They are then sorted by species, size, colour and quality.

➤ **Grading:** This involves evaluation ad gradation of shells on the basis of their quality, completeness, condition, rarity aesthetic appeal and value. High quality shells with minimal damage and imperfections are graded higher.

➤ **Packaging and Storage:** Shells are carefully packed to prevent damage and stored in a controlled environment to preserve their natural quality.

➤ **Wholesale and Retail Marketing:** Shells are sold to wholesalers, who then distribute them to retailers, craft suppliers and online platforms of marketing / sale.

➤ **Crafting and Decoration,** Shells are used in jewellery making, ornaments, dolls, decorative articles, wind chimes etc.

➤ **Global Trading** (Export and Import). Shells are traded globally with many countries, in addition to the local trades and trade within the country.

**Artificial manufacture and production of shells:** Artificial sea-shells mimic the appearance and texture of natural shells; however they lack the unique characteristics lustre and beauty of natural seashells. The man-made shells are used in the following applications such as:- Decorative articles, Architectural features, Industrial uses and scientific research.

The following technological processes are utilized in generating artificial seashells viz. 3-D technology / printing, ceramics, glassblowing, resin casting and composite materials like fibreglass and resin both for industrial and ornamental / decorative purposes.

<u>Conclusion:</u> I am always amazed to see the designs and patterns of seashells, some as huge as conchs, the medium sized humped *cowrie* like shells to tiny ones which were once upon a time used as currency in our country. The amazing world of seashells is as diverse as the moods, emotions and characters of human beings. Here are three stories that show characters as resilient as the sea shell. I dedicate this versetitled "Perfect Seashells" by Jazeera (June 2014) to all the characters that appear in the ensuing two stories.

## Perfect Seashells

And we went to the sea shore...
Far away from the entire bustling little town
I collected all the seashells; while she collected the perfect ones...
We then filled our bags with a bunch of seashells; but what I collected the most was
a bunch of memories.....

\*\*\*\*\*\*\*\*\*\*\*\*\*\*\*\*\*\*\*\*\*\*\*\*\*\*\*\*\*\*\*\*\*\*\*\*\*\*\*\*\*\*\*\*\*\*

# He Dared To Be a Pied Piper

**Introduction:** There are many people that one comes across during one's life time. Some of them unknowingly leave an impression that lasts lifelong. They may be people from common walks of life, very ordinary people with extraordinary skills of communication. Some of them have had an admirable passion to live, despite challenges, but had the indomitable will to help and serve others in their own way. They were not learned men or women but they had seasoned themselves from their life experiences.

I believe that the common man is true to his beliefs. Many of us regard achievers and star performers and contributors as extraordinary and uncommon men / women. However it is the common man/ woman who transforms into a celebrity by the dint of his / her passion, commitment, consistency and dedication.

This is what this maestro; named *A R Rahman* had quoted in some contest: "*I was a common man. And I will always remain a common man. No amount of stardom will ever consume my soul. Money comes, money goes. Fame comes, fame goes. I believe every human being is a celebrity in their own right*".

***Raam Sewak:*** This story on *Raam Sewak* is dedicated to all the common men who have influenced people in some way or the other with special reference to all those common people who proved to be sources of inspiration to me till this point of my life. I shall first throw some light on how did I get associated with the study of Biology. The history and importance of dissection and how did I get oriented to dissection of plants and animals. Later I shall tell you, how did I get acquainted with *Raam Sewak* and why do I remember him with respect to teaching of Biology as I grew up as a teacher.

During my school days, I developed a natural liking to the discipline named Biology / Life Sciences. I not only loved reading the text book content but also passionately explored articles on animals, plants and human beings. In addition to my teachers and peer mates, I owe my gratitude to all the relevant books in the library at school and my residence for nurturing my passion. I also acknowledge the contribution of articles in magazines like *Soviet Land, Mirror, and Readers' Digest* for shaping my perception and adding value to my knowledge quotient at the secondary and senior secondary stages of learning during my schooling.

This is when I came across articles on the aspects of biography of *Socrates, Plato, Aristotle, Theophrastus, Linnaeus, Lamarck, Charaka, Susruta, Dhanvantri, Varahamihira, Mendel* and many more. Further, when I was in Class XI, we had a text book in English named, *"They dared to be Doctors"* that developed a deep-rooted passion and aspiration to learn more about human biology, plant biology and animal biology.

**History of dissection and importance of dissecting animals and plants in understanding zoology and botany:** *Herophilus* (335 BC-255 BC), The Greek anatomist of *Chalcedon, Egypt* is considered as the Father of Anatomy. He has significantly contributed to the distinguishing blood vessels from nerves and arteries from veins. He has also significantly contributed to the understanding of the anatomy of human brain, eye, liver, reproductive organs and nervous system. *Erasistratus* of *Chios* (3$^{rd}$ century), a student of the former anatomist carried forward the practice of dissection and development of the same. *Claudius Galenus* (129-216 AD) of *Pergamon* (present Turkey) was a Roman / Greek physician, surgeon and philosopher. He dissected mainly on Barbary apes. *Galen* did not have the permission to individually dissect upon human cadavers, thereby he used animals. He asked his students to look at dead gladiators or other bodies as they were quite close to human beings.

*Andreas Vesalius* (1514 - 1564) was an archrival of *Herophilus*. He modified to a great extent the drawings and dissection procedures developed by *Herophilus, Erasistratus* and *Galen*. He is often referred to as a Renaissance physician, because he revolutionized the study of biology and the practice of medicine by his accurate and lucid description of the anatomy of the human body. Basing his observations on the dissections that he himself made, he wrote and illustrated the first comprehensive textbook of anatomy. It is said that *Vesalius* performed dissections with thoroughness unknown until then. Meanwhile, in India with the development of *Ayurveda / Ayurvigyana*; *Charaka Samhita, Susruta Samhita* and *Ashtanga Sangraha* laid the foundation to the study of medical sciences and human anatomy. *Susruta* (disciple of *Dhanavantri*) is thereby regarded as the 'founder of *shalyachikitsa*' or the 'father of surgery'. He developed this science about 2000 years ago at *Kashi*.

Thus, study of internal organization of plants, animals and human beings developed as the science of anatomy. This later diversified into incorporate histology (study of tissue composition), cytology / cell biology (cellular composition) and genetics (transmission of genes / molecules of inheritance). Thus, dissection of plants and animals was incorporated at school and college level to relate better to the theoretical basis of study of internal organization.

**My experience with dissection of plants and animals:** The primary thought of cutting fresh plants, their parts and animals did baffle me as I found it quite heinous, especially with animals. My school bag got richer with a dissection box that contained a razor, a pair of scissors, two pairs of forceps, needle pins mounted on plastic, spatula, glass slides, cover glass, cover slips, cotton swab and long pins that could penetrate into wax.

Unfortunately we were never oriented to wearing masks and rubber / plastic hand gloves, while dissecting animals, although we were strictly monitored on having our finger nails trimmed and washing our hands with the then popular antiseptic *Dettol* and *Lifebuoy* soap. Further, we always wore a white apron coat, whenever, we had a Laboratory Class for practical training in Physics,

Chemistry and Biology. I was first oriented to dissect the chloroformed insect-the cockroach (*Periplanata americana*). Prior to this experience, I would always shriek, whenever I had spotted this insect. The laboratory assistant cajoled us into holding the insect and examining its morphology well. He added that this insect has survived for a period of more than 300 million years on this planet, whereas we have lived for about 2.5 million years only. He also said that this insect has survived under extreme situations viz. the dropping of the atom bombs in *Hiroshima and Nagasaki*!

My classmate promptly interjected, *"What about mosquitoes, Sir?"* The lab assistant replied, *"They came much later about 125 million to 200 million years ago. Further they do not have a tough exoskeleton as cockroaches have".*

I got to differentiate between the dorsal and ventral surface of the insect, understand well the segmentation of its body into the head, thorax and the abdomen, why was it an arthropod and the chitin rich waterproof exoskeleton that accounted for its colour and toughness. I gradually got over my aversion in handling the insect and practised to locate the wings, separate the mouth parts, the salivary gland apparatus, the alimentary canal with the set of Malphigiian tubules and the nervous system of the organism.

The second animal that we were given to dissect was the earthworm (*Pheretima posthuma*). The long slimy cylindrical invertebrate, termed as a representative of annelid, had no limbs. Despite the absence of limbs it was well adapted to move within the soil and loosen it. In comparison to the cockroach the dissection of this bisexual animal seemed quite complicated. All the organs were much tinier in proportion. It was with focus and dexterity that one could locate and observe the various pores on its body, chaetae / setae and the reproductive organs and system. An organism with more than 100 segments had well developed alimentary canal and blood vessels. What we had read in theory was well illustrated when we ventured into dissecting this animal bearing rings or annuli.

The third animal that we dissected at school stage was a vertebrate; an amphibian, the frog (*Rana tigrina*). Although the lab assistant handed over each one of us a chloroformed frog; we could well observe that the frog had inflated lungs and was breathing subtly. We could practically understand that why vertebrates are dissected open from the ventral side, along the mid-ventral line, unlike the invertebrates that are cut open along the mid-dorsal line. There was a lot of peer learning happening during practical classes.

During graduation, I gained the experience of dissecting the following invertebrates in addition to the three mentioned in the earlier paragraphs viz. the annelid clam worm *Nereis*, the bivalve mollusc and the water mussel (*Unio*), the gastropod apple snail (*Pila*). Further among vertebrates we mastered the dissection of the dog fish (*Scoliodon*), the wall lizard (*Hemidactylus*) and the pigeon (*Columba livia*). During post-graduation we worked with ecological impact on insects, annelids and molluscs and physiological experiments with frogs and rats (*Rattus rattus*).

The word dissection is more often and naturally associated with animals and animal parts, however what was dissected in plants? It was generally the flower and its parts viz. calyx, corolla, the male reproductive whorl or the *androecium* and the female reproductive whorl or the *gynoecium*. We would take thin transverse (slices) and longitudinal sections of the stem and root and prepare stained slides under the dissecting microscope. In addition, there were numerous physiological experiments that involved potted plants and plant parts viz, twigs and root systems.

**When did I come across *Raam Sewak?*** As I joined the teaching profession in a senior secondary school, in a steel township, named *Bhilai*, in the erstwhile state of *Madhya Pradesh*. I realised my role as a teacher. The onus and responsibility of imparting the right learning lay upon me both as a Biology teacher and as an individual. I realised that I may not have been an extraordinary performer as a student; however, I needed to be an excellent teacher, reaching out to every student. Thereby I tried my best to blend practical with theory in addition to the Board prescribed practical work.

The Board had prescribed the dissection of rat for Senior Secondary Classes. Each Class had more than forty students. Demonstration of dissection was not sufficient. Students needed practice at least twice during the year to develop and demonstrate their skills of dissection of rats and knowledge of the body systems and correlate to human body systems in presence of the external examiner appointed by the Board.

White rats (*Rattus norvegicus*) were rarely available; black rats (*Rattus rattus*) were more commonly found. Yet who would trap them? Individual rat traps could entrap just one or two rodents. Neither the lab attendants nor the peons could collect the required number of rats.

The steel township had more than fifteen schools. Each school had a recurring requirement of living rats. Some of these schools had about 75-80 students. In other words the demand for rats was quite high and almost at the same time of the year viz. July- August i.e. prior to the first term, December- January which was prior to the second term and March during Board Exams. Fortunately, there was a nexus amongst the Biology Teachers and Principals of majority of the steel township schools. One of them suggested the name of *Raam Sewak* and his contact details.

Thus, *Raam Sewak* came into picture. At the first meeting I found him to be quite loud and garrulous. He was quite clumsily dressed with unkempt hair. He wore loose *hawai chappals* (flip flops). He was holding a cage with 8-10 healthy white rats (marketing strategy). He had also brought along with him a document quoting the price of white rats and black rats (quotation). I was curious to know about him and his occupation and thereby I asked him.

That's when he said that he was earlier working as a member in the artillery corps in the Indian army. Thereby he could handle guns and weapons. I was doubtful as his physique and demeanour did not make me believe the fact. His father, who was a native of *Durg*, Madhya Pradesh, passed away. Being the only son, he had to shoulder the responsibility of the family. Thereby he quit the services and returned to *Durg*. After some time he joined as a laboratory attendant in the Botany Department of the Government Arts and Science College, *Durg*. He also mentioned that he had set up a shop for his sons at *Durg*. The shop dealt with the sale / supply of scientific instruments and chemicals. He pointed out that the quotation had the name and address of the shop. He also handed over an off-white soiled visiting card on which was printed the names of his sons and the same address and contact number. In those days only BSNL land line numbers existed.

He made it very clear that this was a venture that he had started to supplement his income. His boys were not trained to trap rats. It was he himself who set traps in fields, godowns, granaries and grocery shops. He did this job after he got free from his college. Since he was a government employee, the venture was in the name of his sons, who were yet to be groomed. My senior in the Biology Department was quite sceptical and asked if he would really be able to cater to the requirements and deliver the rats on time and as and when required.

He took out a folded exercise book from the pocket of his trousers. I noticed that this note-book served as his diary. He showed about 25 entries against specific dates over the previous three months. The specifications mentioned his supply details to different schools. He then held out the cage in front of us and said in Hindi, *"Madam aapne verbally Sector IV School ke Sir ko apna requirement batlaaya thha, aur yeh dekhiye main laaya nahin kya? Abhi tak maine unnko nahin supply kiya hai. Aap ko daene ke baad unnko doonga. Baahar gaadi mein rakhi hui hai ek aur pinjra. Bharosa rakhiye main zimmedaar vyakti hoon, Aazma kar to dekhiye!"*

Translation of what he said, *"Madam you had verbally informed the teacher of Sector IV School about your requirement, and look did I not promptly fetch you your requirement? I have not yet supplied him; I shall be doing so after I hand you over your requirement. The cage with rats meant for that school is kept out in my vehicle. Trust me, I am a responsible person and try me out"*

He kept the cage on the Biology lab platform, grinned at the lab attendant and students sitting in the laboratory. He sped back to the gate, where he had parked his vehicle. Thus, students dissected the white rats after they were chloroformed,

This was how; *Raam Sewak* first entered our school to supply rats. One of the students commented, *"Mam! Doesn't he remind us of the character The Pied Piper of Hamelin?* True enough. The illustration of the strange looking man named ***Pied Piper*** in the English text book along with the story depicted the man who played the pipe and walked along the roads of *Hamelin.* He was followed by all the rats of *Hamelin*, was unbelievably akin to the physiognomy of Raam Sewak. The peculiar appearance, the long aquiline nose, broad eyes and the forehead were so very similar. Only thing that *Raam Sewak's* dress and the pointed hat of the fictitious *Pied Piper* were different. This made me wonder, how could the illustrator of a story written by Grimm Brothers and Robert Browning imagine the Pied Piper, so similar to *Raam Sewak* or was it a mere coincidence.

***Raam Sewak's* commitment:** The *Pied Piper* of the original tale was committed to his work and as he had promised the king of *Hamelin* to remove all the rats from the rat infested town of *Hamelin*. He played such a strange tune on his pipe that all the rats that had plagued the town, followed him as though they were hypnotized; until all of them drowned in the river in the outskirts of *Hamelin*.

I wondered what kind of lute *Raam Sewak* had to play to trap at a time a minimum 500 rats, to cater to all the schools at a time. We would always be anxious and tense till the last moment keeping our fingers crossed such that *RaamSewak* took care of our requirement. Although it appeared that he would dilly-dally, he would always reach at the eleventh hour, with his grin and guffaw, to provide us the rodents for dissection. This was his reputation at other schools as well.

Further, he had a monopoly in this trade, although it was in no way lucrative. He would also supply frogs, cockroaches and earthworms for the secondary classes. Our School Principal found him to be quite committed, although in the first meeting with him, he was taken aback by his brashness and his apparent uncouth appearance.

In this context, here's a couplet by *Sant Kabir*:

**नहाये धोये क्या हुआ, जो मन मैल न जाये।**
**मीन सदा जलमें रहे, धोये बास न जाये।।**

*(NahayeDhoye)* a bath that washes and cleanses the body; (*Kya hua*) what is the outcome? (*mann maiyl*) bad thoughts in the mind maligned mind; (*Jo na jaaye*) that does not cleanse, wash or remove; (*Meen sadaaa*) the fish that always; (*Jal men rahe*) lives / remains in water, (*Dhoyeye*) when washed; (*baas na jaaye)* the stink / bad odour continues to linger on / canot be removed.

The external appearance of an individual does not make much of a difference. What matters the most is how one as a person is? Beautiful faces may be deceptive; however one cannot be deceived by the beauty of robust and healthy minds.

Thus as long as I was in this school and moved on to the next, I happened to meet periodically meet Raam Sewak and was always amused by the anecdotes that he narrated. He was the same from the first day till the last day that I met him. There was no change in him, be it his attire or footwear. He never put on airs nor was bound to any kind of egotism. He continued to do his work, trying his best to fulfill the needs of one and all!

***************************************************

# *Spring Tides and Neap Tides*

**Introduction:** It was the 13<sup>th</sup> of May, 2019, *Shrimati Antima Das,* a retired English professor, aged 69, who was travelling by train No. 18409, *Jagannath Express*, woke up with a start. She glanced at her wrist-watch. It was 2:30 a.m. The train was moving quite fast. It was quite dark. It was sufficient for her to figure out the details of the coupe and the compartment with the light being emitted from the lamp on the ceiling of the corridor of the train compartment; between the six berths and two of the side berths.

She was in the lower berth of the 3 tier AC Compartment, thereby was not able to sit up straight, as the occupied middle berth was quite low and proved to be a hindrance for her to sit upright. Anyway, without causing disturbance to the fellow passengers, she managed to adjust the soft pillows that were issued by the railway authorities thereby, raise her head and stretch out her legs. She closed her eyes, although she realised that she would never be able to sleep once she had woken up. Since she was travelling, she preferred not to have that day, the prescribed sleeping pills prescribed by her doctor, although she consumed the anti-depressant pills as a ritual.

She had boarded the train at *Shalimar* Junction on the previous evening. The train started at 7:30p.m. and was scheduled to reach *JagannathPuri*, next day early in the morning by 4:30 a.m. Soon after the train left *Shalimar* after a few stations it eternally stopped for about two hours at *Belda* on account of some technical reasons. All the passengers tended to curse the government, the people associated with the railways and as well as their stars. *AntimaDas* was amused to overhear their conversation, although she did not participate in the conversation. She preferred to read the book that she had with her. She had borrowed this book titled *Skin in the Game* from her student *Manikankana*. However she could not concentrate in reading the book and kept flipping the pages and browsing. Coincidentally she came across the following lines in the book by *Nassim Nicholas Taleb* that seemed to be so relevant to the situation.

The lines read as follows: *"The curse of modernity is that we are increasingly populated by a class of people who are better at explaining than understanding, or better at explaining than doing."*

As the train did not move for about two hours, the air conditioners were not functional. It was terribly humid and hot. Soon after the train moved out from *Belda* station; passengers went to sleep. It was ten minutes past midnight. As the passengers in her coupe were settling down to sleep they mentioned to each other that the train was expected to reach *Jagannath Puri*onlyby 6:30 a.m. *Antima* switched off the reading light above her head, plugged her cell-phone to the plug-point available in the train coupe. She said her prayers and closed her eyes in an effort to sleep. Although *Antima* had closed her eyes; it took her a long time almost 45 minutes for her to sleep. It was barely two hours that she had slept and now she was broad awake at 2:30 a.m.

**Memories pleasant and unpleasant:** She tried to divert herself by mentally following the rhythm of the train moving on the rails, indulging in backward counting. The fact that 'now, she was left all alone', kept haunting her! Neither could she stop remembering, one by one: her grandfather, her parents, her siblings, her maternal uncle, her husband, his son and daughter, her brother-in-law and his wife.Nor could she restrain the flow of thoughts that flooded her mind, resulting in tears in her eyes.

*Childhood, full of bliss:* Antima was the fourth and the last child, born in the year 1950, to *Gopal Das* and *Mrunmayee*. *Gopal's* father, *Atulananda Das* who was addressed by his grandchildren as *Thakuda*; was the senior most member of the family. All the seven members of the family lived in this small thatched ancestral house in a coastal village named *Mandarmani*, located in the *Purba Mednipur* district in *West Bengal*.

*Shri Atulananda* had inherited from his father, *Shri Gokulananda Das*; a small piece of agricultural land, a small house and the skills to accept challenges and lead a content life. *Atulananda's* occupation was farming and fishing. *Gopal Das* was his only son. Three years after *Gopal* was born, *Atulananda's* wife *Sraboni* passed away as she became a victim to a mysterious disease, which had taken toll of many lives in the coastal village. On the death of his wife, *Atulananda* had taken the vow of celibacy and he brought up his son all alone.

*Gopal* studied in the government school of *Digha*, which was about 17 Kms. from his ancestral village, *Mandarmani*. *Gopal* was a brilliant student. He topped the *Madhyamik* (high school) examination. *Atulananda* was very proud of his son, especially when he received his first gold medal in academics from his school. *Gopal* desired to pursue his graduation from Presidency College, *Calcutta*. However, he had to be content with pursuing his studies in the Government College located in the suburbs of *Calcutta*. His subjects were English, *Bengali*, Political Science, History and Economics. Later, during post graduation, he pursued his studies in English as he had a flair and strong liking for the language. He qualified an examination and was selected for the post of head-master. It was coincidental that the government had established a primary and a secondary school at village *Mandarmani*.

Thus *Gopal Das* became the headmaster of the village school. He was happy that the children of his native village would not have to face all the hardships and challenges that he had faced just because there was no school in the village during his years of schooling.

*Gopal Das* was quite popular in thevillage as the school head-master. His wife was *Mrunmayee* whom he had married when she was 16 and he was 20. *Mrunmayee* spent her entire life in *'Thakursewa'* (service to Lord Krishna), taking care of the house, cooking, washing and nurturing, her sons: *Krishnendu* and *Bimalendu* and younger daughters *Arunima* and *Antima*. The siblings were born at intervals of two years each. Thus when *Antima* was 6 years' old, *Arunima* was 8 years of age, *Bimalendu* was 10 years old and *Krishnendu* was 12 years of age. All of them were greatly adored by their grandfather *Atulananda* and their parents.

The horn of a fast moving train woke *Antima* from her reverie. She once again glanced at her watch. It was just 3:15 a.m. She realized that there were further three hours left for her to reach her destination, *Jagannath Puri*. She closed her eyes and recalled the association with her elder brothers (*daada*) and elder sister (*didi*)

**Academic and career pursuit of the *Das* siblings:** All the four brothers and sisters completed their schooling from the secondary school at *Mandarmani*.

***Krishnendu's academic pursuit:*** Her elder brother *Krishnendu* was a brilliant student. He was an idealist and strictly followed the instructions and guidelines of his grandfather and parents. He was very sharp in Mathematics and Sciences. He aimed to become an astrophysicist. Thereby he was focussed to qualify the IIT entrance and pursue his passion at one of the top Universities in USA.

***Bimalendu's rebellious attitude:*** *Bimalendu dada* was not very passionate with studies. He was more into football and athletics. When at school he did qualify for the State Level Athletics and win a few medals in sprint events, discus, shot-put and javelin throws. He desired that soon after schooling he should join the *Mohun Bagan*

*Athletics Club* at *Kolkata*. But he was inconsistent. He proved to be a rebel and as he grew into an adolescent, he would always try to violate all the necessary rules to lead a disciplined way of life.

At school, he hated the system of examinations. In order to avoid appearing exams he initially would feign that he was sick, later he started bunking school. In the company of a few friends (sons of rich fathers) of distant *mohallas*, whom he had met during the Under-16 State Athletic Meet, he picked up the vices of smoking and drinking liquor. He would be punished at school by his teachers' and his father would support their stand. Thereby the younger son started disliking his father, all the more.

He cared a foot for all the guidance and advices given by his grandfather and mother. Many a time he would become very rude and at times, violent with his elder brother. He scorned at his mother's advice and paid no heed to what she advised. He also lent deaf ears to the opinion of his sisters *Arunima* and *Antima*, as he loathed them and was always disrespectful to them or the other girls of the society. He would often pick up bitter arguments with his father, because his father wanted his son to outshine in academics as his elder brother. *Bimalendu* thus started harbouring hatred and ill-will against his *'dada' Krishnendu*. His arrogant and waylaid behaviour was always the cause of anxiety for the family.

***Moments of pride:*** Meanwhile, at the age of 18, *Krishnendu* cracked the IIT entrance and joined IIT,

*Kharagpur* to pursue technical Degree Courses in Astrophysical Sciences. This was a moment of pride for the family. *Bimalendu* was further irked by his brother's achievement; he then longed to prove his worth to his family members and the society by hook or crook.

***Moments of anxiety and grief:*** Two years later, on the advice of his rich friends, who had convinced him that he had a bright future at Calcutta; *Bimalendu* planned to run away from home. On the last day of the State Board Examination, he fled away from school with his mother's jewellery and cash that he had managed to smuggle the previous night. The family was shattered.

*Atulananda* and his son *Gopal Das* were consumed with grief, fury and worry. Grandfather did not utter a word after this instance; and he confined himself to the shed in the open space in the backyard. *Gopal Das* worked mechanically. A day after a long search he lodged a complaint with the local police, stating that his younger son had gone missing. He was shameful to face the school community and many a time questioned his conscience, as to, where did he go wrong in parenting his younger son? All their efforts in locating him to bring him back home were in vain.

***Grandfather passes away:*** A week later, early in the morning, *Thakurda Atulananda* was found dead in his cot in the shed in the backyard. Grief had probably consumed his life. *Krishnendu* came down from *Kharagpur* for the funeral. *Gopal Das* and *Mrunmayee* were hopeful that *Bimalendu* would return home on somehow getting the news of the death of his grandfather. Lo! *Bimalendu* never returned home. *Mrunmayee* longed for his arrival and grew melancholic. *Antima* was also deeply affected, although she kept herself busy with her school activities and tasks.

*Krishnendu* pacified his family members, during this visit. He asked his mother to have faith in her daily prayers and seek solace in *Thakur Sewa*. He still believed that destiny surely must have better plans for *Bimalendu*. He told his mother, "*Look ma! Bimal, your prodigal son shall one day return home with awakening and realization and shall prove to be yourworthiest son*".

***Krishnendu's dream comes true:*** Three years later, at the age of 23 by the dint of his efforts he joined the University of California at Berkley to pursue his higher studies in astrophysics. This was yet another moment for *GopalDas*, his wife and daughters to take pride in the achievement of their elder son.

***Time flies faster than lightning:*** *Mrunmayee* wondered at the unimaginable pace at which time had sped past! Now her sons were of the age 23 and 21, while the daughters were 19 and 17 respectively. It struck her that she and her husband would have to very soon hunt for suitable matches for their daughters.

***Arunima's career pursuit:*** Soon after the declaration of the school final results, at the age of 17, *Arunima* joined a private women's college at *Digha*. Her father had accompanied her and all her six school friends to the college, on the day of admission to the graduation courses. He was amazed to see the tall three storey building of the Women's College and so were all the seven girls from *Mandarmani!* *Arunima* and three of her classmates sought enrolment into graduation courses in Commerce; while the other three sought admission into Humanities.

*Arunima* felt very happy to move out from her village. She had never moved out of the village, for the past seventeen years. She realized that it would be fun to study in a college in this busy township, which happened to be always crowded as it was a tourist resort as well. She thus along with her six schoolmates, began commuting to *Digha*, on all weekdays (except Sundays) by the state transport bus at 8:30 a.m. from the village bus stand to the College Square of the town. They would return to their village by the 5:30 p.m. bus, in case they missed this bus service there was the last bus that would reach them by 6:30 p.m.

***Experiences at the College Campus:*** *Arunima* felt like a free bird! She was amazed to note there were 120 girls in the Commerce Class and about 125 in the Humanities Section. The building catering to the B.Sc. courses was at a 15 minute walk-distance with well equipped laboratories and Lecture Halls. She was amused that despite being teenagers, girls of the college being addressed as ladies / women. And probably to pronounce the fact all the students had to wear to college, the traditional Indian attire, sari with blouse. *Arunima*, thereby cajoled her mother to part with the best of her saris / drapery and she fondly wore them to college.

She was very impressed by her College Principal, *Smt. Shyamali Mukherjee* and all the lady professors. *Arunima* and all her six mates from her school were termed as the 'ladies from *Mandarmani*' at the college. The College Library was huge and impressive building with a large Reference Section and a larger Reading Room. The hawk eyed Senior Librarian *Smt. Chanchala Ghosh* was a strict lady. She was usually found pacing up and down the Library supervising the students in the library as well as the six Junior Librarians under her charge.

***Extravaganza:*** The college building had a beautiful garden, with rows of *Ashoka* trees along the compound wall. There was a large banyan tree on one end, under which were a dozen round tables made of bamboo with chairs all around. Students sat there during their free periods. Some discussed their lessons, a would be busy taking down notes, while a few more would be busy pulling each others' legs, cracking jokes and gossiping about their favourite movies, movie stars.

Another area where the students, especially the second year and third year students would throng was the College Canteen. The canteen was popular for the following dishes: *Singhada, Aloo chop, Luchi tarkari, Koraishtir Kachouri, Ghugni* available in addition to sweetmeats viz. *Jilepi, Rosogolla, Sandesh, Paeda, Mihidaana,* along with *Chanchur* and tea. A combination of these popular Bengali *naashta* would be served every alternate day / week. For example: *Aloochop, Singhada* and *Jilepi* on one day, *Luchi tarkari, Ghugni* and *Sandesh* on the other day and so on.

***Winds of change:*** All went well with *Arunima* in the first year and first half of the second year of graduation. All that while, she would narrate during dinner time at home to her father, mother and sister, *Antima* all that had happened during the day at the college as well as amusing anecdotes during their to and fro bus trips.

When, *Antima*, wasin the second year of graduation there was a new entrant, by the name *Shahina*. She had joined midway by virtue of her brother's transfer from Calcutta. *Shahina* was quite bold and modern in her outlook. Gradually, *Arunima* and *Shahina* developed a very strong bond of friendship. *Shahina* once casually introduced *Arunima* her cousin *Rizwaan*. She told her that he had his own business at *Digha*. He generally came down along with *Shahina* by his van to drop her at the college and at times fetch her.

***Noticeable behavioural changes in Arunima:*** She started avoiding her six friends from *Mandarman*. When this happened quite often with them, they were very disturbed and hurt by her avoidance. She would invariably avail the last bus and reach home late. At times, her friend's cousin *Rizwaan* would drop her at the village bus stop by his van, travelling from *Digha* to *Mandarmani*.

*Arunima* was greatly impressed by the looks, mannerism and attire of *Rizwaan*. After a couple of such meetings, *Rizwaan*, *Shahina* and *Arunima* ventured to move about together in the van and visit the beachside. Obviously, *Shahina* and *Antima* would stealthily move out of the college after attending the first period at college.

*Rizwaan* would be waiting with his van near the bus stop. *Shahina* seemed to play the role of a Good Samaritan to both of them. She had further taken up the role of fanning the flames of infatuation in *Arunima* that gradually blossomed to love. Gradually, *Arunima* started moving out to places viz.cinema hall, restaurant, and shanty resorts with *Rizwaan* alone.

At home she was found to be tight-lipped and day dreaming. She seldom spoke to her parents or sister as she spoke to them earlier. She started hiding facts and things. *Rizwaan* had gifted her numerous fancy items in order to woe her. She was always worried that no one in the family should get any inkling about the gifts and the spot where she had hidden them. Further, she was worried that if her parents would get to know about her relationship with *Rizwaan*, they would never accept him as he belonged to a different community and followed the *Islamic* religion. She would flare up and get annoyed whenever her parents spoke about values, ethics and idealism.

***Unexpected turn that causes turmoil:*** It was Friday evening. Headmaster *Gopal Das* had returned home. *Mrunmayee* offered the *sandhyadeep / diya* and hailed the good spirits, gods and goddesses by blowing the traditional conch / *shankh*. *Antima* was busy kneading the dough for preparing *ruti/ rotis* for dinner. The pendulum clock on the wall chimed seven times, indicating that it was seven o'clock. *Gopal Das* glanced at his wrist watch and called out to his wife questioning her whether *Arunima* had returned from the college. *Mrunmayee*, indicated that she had not returned as yet. *Gopal Das* rose up from his easy-chair, picked up the torch and said to his wife, "*Let me go to the bus-stop and find out, if the last bus from Digha has arrived.*" He put on his sandals and walked to the bus-stand.

A few people on the way accosted him. Headmaster *Gopal Das* mechanically accosted them in return. He found no one seated in the bus-stand. There were a few people at Uttam's *paan*-shop. He went up to the small *paan*-shop and asked *Uttam* the shopkeeper if the last bus had arrived. He replied, "*Meshomoshai* last bus *saadhe chho taye eshe giyechhilo, aar Digha phiregaelo!*"

*[(*Meshomoshai*) Uncle / gentleman, (*saadhe chho taye*) at six thirty, (*eshe giye chhilo*) last bus had arrived, (*aar Digha phire gaelo*) and the last bus has returned to Digha]*

The headmaster grew anxious. He walked aimlessly on the road for some time. Then, he recalled about *Kakoli Choudhury*, one of *Arunima's* friends, who was pursuing graduation in Sciences from the same college. He decided to find out from her about his daughter, *Arunima*. He went up to her house. Her father, *Jiten Choudhury*, a contractor by profession was at the gate. He was surprised and happy to see the school headmaster, *Shri Gopal Das* approaching his residence. He invited him in and he called aloud for his daughter, "*Kakoli! O ma Kakoli!, daekho toh ke aesechaen aamadaer ghoare!*" *[O ma Kakoli= My dear Kakoli ! daekho toh= look / see, ke aesechaen= who has come, aamadaer ghoare!=to our house!]*

105

***In search of Arunima:*** The headmaster realized that the moods prevailing in him and *Kakoli's* father was diabolically opposite. He felt hesitant to express his anxiety. On seeing *Kakoli*, he mustered some strength and asked him whether his daughter *Arunima* was there with her and other mates, in the bus, while returning from the college. She replied point blank, *"No!"* She added that for the past fortnight, *Arunima*, no doubt, commuted with them from the village bus-stand to the College Square at *Digha* but had never accompanied them, while returning from *Digha* College Square to *Mandarmani* bus stand.

*Gopal Das* was puzzled by *Kakoli's* version. He thought for a while, recalling that for the past fortnight he had seen his daughter arrive always at home latest by 6:45 p.m. He spoke aloud his observation and asked *Kakoli* how did *Arunima* then commute and reach home on time, although she did not commute by the last bus? After hesitating for a while, she spoke in a timid voice that she preferred to travel from *Digha* to *Mandarmani* with *Rizwaan* on his bike, rather than the bus. This information was like a bolt from the blue! The headmaster said, "*Ki boalchho tumi ma!*" *["What are you telling, my dear?"]* *"Who is this Rizwaan?"* *Kakoli* spoke out whatever she knew. She also mentioned that after having become friends with *Shahina* and *Rizwaan*; *Arunima* rarely spoke to the group of six of her schoolmates from *Mandarmani*.

This was all news for *Gopal Das*. He wondered why *Arunima* had never mentioned about these two friends.

Overhearing the conversation between the headmaster and his daughter, *Kakoli, Jiten Choudhury* could sense that there was some sensitive matter brewing up. He tried to ease the situation asking *Gopal Das* to have tea that was prepared by and was being served by his wife *Shanti*. He reluctantly had a few sips of tea that was served. He was quite confused and tense.

He got up saying, *"Let me find out where my daughter, Arunima is?"* He reached home, where *Mrunmayee* and *Antima* were anxiously waiting for him to arrive. *Gopal Das* was dejected to note that *Arunima* had not yet arrived home. He narrated half-heartedly about whatever information that he had received from *Kakoli*. He also enquired them that if at any point of time *Arunima* had mentioned to them about *Shahina* or *Rizwaan*?

*Antima* went in to her elder sister's study table. She tried opening the drawer and found that it was locked. There were a few books lying on the table. She checked in and flicked through all the pages of the reference books. She could just find *Arunima's* library card and a few loose sheets with scribbles and doodles. *Gopal Das* recalled that during *Arunima's* admission, the College Principal, *Smt. Shyamali Mukherjee* had handed over to him her visiting card with her telephone numbers of both her office and residence.

After rummaging through the papers in his table drawer, he could locate the visiting card. The telephone at his home had the STD facility. In anticipation that the College Principal would be at home he rang her up. The phone kept on ringing but there was no response. At his third attempt, there was someone at the other end who kept repeating in *Bangla*, "*Hello! Ke? Hello! Who's that?*" *Gopal Das* asked for the lady / the College Principal. The person on the other side replied that he was the man-servant of the house and the Principal had gone out to attend a wedding at Calcutta. She was expected to return on the day after the next day. Before *Arunima's* father could ask for anything else he disconnected the call. The clock chimed twelve. It was midnight and the wait for *Arunima* continued to be unduly long! There was no trace of her. It was a grueling night for *Gopal Das*, *Mrunmayee* and *Antima!*

*__Traumatic experience:__* The next two days Saturday and Sunday; *Gopal Das* was on his toes. He ran from pillar to post in search of his daughter. He went to *Digha* College. He met *Arunima's* professors, classmates, whomsoever possible. *Shahina* was not present in the college. He managed to get Shahina's contact address from the College enrolment register and went to the address. It was a small house located near a resort of *Digha*. However the house was locked.

Neighbours said that six months earlier a couple had come down from *Calcutta* and were living together. The people around believed that they were husband and wife. They were seldom indoors as they kept moving in a van, majority of the time. On Saturday evening, *Gopal Das* lodged a complaint about her missing daughter, at *Digha* police station after he had spoken to the SI at the police station of *Mandarmani*. Where was *Arunima* then? How could she vanish into thin air? *Gopal Das* was mentally devastated and physically exhausted.

The police started their investigation. They had a session with the College Principal and her professors. The professors said that *Arunima* was undoubtedly a bright student, however for the past nine months, she was quite distracted. Further she was attending only one period in a day for the past five months. This was yet another shock for headmaster *Gopal Das*. The police also enquired all her six friends from *Mandarmani*; especially about *Shahina* and *Rizwaan*. The news spread like wildfire at *Mandarmani*. When the police came into *Gopal Das's* house to investigate and search through all the belongings of *Arunima*, *Mrunmayee* was very upset. Further, when they broke open the locked drawer and trunk of *Arunima*; she was aghast to find that as a mother she was unaware that her daughter had so many gifts from both *Shahina* and *Rizwaan* in possession with her. How come her daughter had become so secretive? What was wrong with her parenting that *Arunima* preferred to alienate herself from her parents and sister? The police wanted to find a clue about the true identities of *Shahina* and *Rizwaan*, however they were clueless.This incident was a second blow to the family after *Bimalendu* had absconded. This time, both the parents were almost smashed to smithereens.

***A mystery forever:*** With the passage of time one day after the other, one week after the other; *Gopal Das*, *Mrunmayee* and *Antima* kept longing for the return of

*Arunima*, all in vain. The police started reporting to *Gopal Das* about cases of dead bodies (of *Arunima's* age) being recovered from unknown sites after suspected suicides / homicides / accidents, he would shudder and visit the spots. On one end, it would be a great relief for him to find that it was not *Arunima*; however on the other end his anxiety increased manifold. *Mrunmayee* was periodically fainting and she fell into fits of rage and hysteria. The doctor put her on sleeping pills as she had not slept over many nights. *Antima* had to take charge of her mother and the entire house. One night, she was dismayed to see her father bitterly crying. She had always witnessed him as a stern and strict headmaster and undoubtedly as a loving and caring father. She had to console him, although she herself was gradually getting bogged down in a quagmire of depression.

**The train reaches *Jagannath Puri* and school-mates meet after four decades**: As the train bustled into *Jagannath Puri* Railway Station, *Antima's* chain of thoughts broke and she realized that it was 6:45 a.m. She gathered her belongings and shoved them into her tote bag. She had a trolley suitcase. Her school-mate *Sanchita* from *Mandarmani* was there to receive her at the *Puri* Railway Station. She was clad in the white (dress code of *Brahmakumaris sevika*). They were meeting after more than four decades. *Sanchita* was her only class-mate who was in touch with *Antima*; whenever she was in depression or mental turmoil she would be there to counsel her through her letters and periodic telephone calls.

*Sanchita* was at an important position at the *Brahmakumaris Puri Retreat Centre* also known as Godly *Rajayoga* Retreat Centre. She had arranged for a session for *Antima* at the centre. As they travelled in a van, to the centre they exchanged a lot of smiles however could not speak much as they used to during schooling; they realized that they had grown quite old. The cool pure air and placid environment gave *Antima* a feeling of immense peace and solitude which proved to be ideal for introspection and reflection that was crucial for the spiritual journey that she intended to partake with the advice and guidance of *Sanchita*.

The retreat centre provided separate rooms for the participants. *Sanchita* led *Antima* to her accommodation, ensured that she was comfortable. She handed over the schedule of the programme for the retreat scheduled from the next day over a period of seven days. She hugged her. Before leaving she said, *"As per the rules of the centre we have all the three meals at the dining hall. Breakfast is over by 7:30 a.m. That's why I had arranged for the breakfast to be kept on your table. I will be busy till 1:30 p.m. You can relax until then. Watch the sea that is just across your window. I shall come down to fetch you. We shall have lunch together and catch up with all that we have missed out. Antima thanks for coming down. You are a bold woman. You shall be a stronger person after the initiation and the seven day Raja Yoga. Life is certainly challenging. It's always turbulent. It's full of tides. The Universe always provides us the strength to meet all the challenges and so shall you!"* Antima had her bath, followed by breakfast. She sat at the window sill watching the waves of the sea. The rays of the morning sun glowed as golden strands that broke with rising waves and fell in place as the waves receded. In this process she once again started travelling down the memory lane, from the point where she left.

*Krishnendu* visits his family: Six months had passed away after *Arunima* had disappeared, when *Krishnendu* arrived. He was aware about all the happenings. *Antima* was in the habit of writing posting him a letter, once a month. During those days, overseas telephonic conversation was quite costly and dearer. His heart bled to see the condition of his parents. He was undoubtedly, quite close to his parents, *Bimalendu* and both the sisters. He had never wanted to be away from them. However, he was well established and busy with his projects and as a professional that he was not able to abandon his passion and come down to India immediately.

He was pained and sad to see that life of his parents and *Antima* had come to almost a standstill. It seemed that it was an eternal wait for *Bimalendu* and *Arunima* whereas the siblings had no heart to retun home. He was also unhappy to see that amidst all this chaos, *Antima* was not able to pursue her studies, after her School Finals. She had always wanted to pursue her studies at *Santiniketan*. Thereby he had called his maternal uncle, *Shyamal Sen* from *Bolpur* town. He arrived a week after *Krishnendu* arrived. He was also taken aback to see the condition of his sister *Mrunmayee* and his stoic brother-in-law, *Gopal Das*.

**Future Plans**: *Krishnendu* had come to India on a leave period of three months. Thereby, he took the lead to talk to his father about getting rid off the mental suffering that they were undergoing. His father expressed that, he no longer wanted to continue with his services as the headmaster of the school, although he had contributed a lot to the development of the school community. After deliberations and counter arguments, it was decided that all the three of them shift to *Bolpur*. It was a very tough and painful decision for the family to leave their native abode.

***Das family shifts from Mandarmani to Bolpur:*** *Shyamal Sen* was a wholesale cloth merchant. *Shyamal* and *Nandini* was a childless couple. *Shyamal's* wife *Nandini* did not approve of her husband being instrumental help shifting his sister, brother-in-law and his daughter from their village *Mandarmani*to *Bolpur* town. On one end she vied for *Krishnendu* as a prospective alliance for her sister's daughter who was at *Kolkata*, just because he was a *'phoren'* settled *chhele* (suitor settled abroad). On the other end she did not want her sister-in-law, *Mrunmayee* or niece, *Antima*, to be granted any kind of favour by her husband, *Shyamal*. *Gokul Das* and his son had foreseen this situation; thereby they had made it clear that they would prefer to stay in a separate house at *Bolpur* without causing aunt *Nandini* any trouble.

***Antima's career pursuit:*** Soon, *Gopal Das* could establish his reputation as an excellent English and Economics teacher, through the tuition centre that he had developed at *Bolpur*. *Antima* was enrolled at *Vishwa Bharati University Shantiniketan*, for pursuing BA Honours in English Literature. *Krishnendu* had made it clear, that he was not interested in getting married until the family had settled well at this new place and *Antima's* wedding was accomplished after she had completed her graduation.

*Krishnendu* flew off to USA after his period of vacation was over. He was worried about his mother's psychological disposition, mental health and physical well being. She was now being treated for hysteria and depression. *Antima* would commute to the University as it was just 3 Kilometres away from *Bolpur* town. *Gopal Das* had taken the responsibility of cooking the morning meals, as *Antima* had her college from 9 a.m. to 4 p.m. He had his tuition classes from 2 p.m. to 8 p.m. in the evening. There was a maid at home to take care of *Mrunmayee* as well as the maintenance of the house.

***The head of the family passes away:*** All went well for about 9 months. *Gopal Das* suffered a cerebral stroke. He was hospitalized for a month and a half after which he passed away. *Krishnendu* flew to India, for performing the final rites. He went back after 12 days. This was again a period of trial for *Antima*. Although, her uncle, *Shyamal* helped her out without the knowledge of his wife, it would often lead to misunderstandings and quarrels between *Nandini* and *Antima*.

On account of her mother's ill health, although she was not able to focus well on her studies, she managed to qualify graduation with flying colours. It was a tight-rope walk for her to complete her post graduation in English from the same University. She also qualified the University Grants Commission National Eligibility Test and thereby qualified as an assistant professor in English. In addition to taking care of her mother and administering medicines on the basis of the monthly check up and prescription; *Antima* kept herself busy throughout the day. She had no other diversion other than her vocation. Although she felt happy teaching and meeting students from diverse backgrounds, a latent depression was setting in her. She did not want to get married, for she was worried about her mother. Because soon after her marriage, it would be expected that she move along with her husband to settle at his place. Then, who would take care of her mother?

***Wedding proposal for Antima:*** When she was 30 years old, her uncle *Shyamal Sen* brought in a wedding alliance from Dr. *Shambhu Dutta* a 38 year old physician. His wife had passed away 6 years earlier. His son and daughter were of 15 and 9 years of age respectively. The doctor was earlier acquainted with *Gopal Das* when he had consulted him with respect to his wife *Mrunmayee's* treatment. Further, he had off late seen *Antima* with *Mrunmayee* at the government hospital when she had brought her mother for the medical check-up.

He was seeking a responsible companion who could also be a good mother to his children. He also knew that *Antima* could never leave her mother alone unattended or at the mercy of others. Thereby he was ready to render proper support to her mother as well. *Shyamal* had briefed *Krishnendu* about this proposal over the telephone. He knew that, as a brother he would object to *Antima* getting married to a person who was already wedded. He arranged for a virtual meeting of *Krishnendu* with *Dr. Shambhu* over Skype. *Krishnendu* took into account different perspectives and was convinced that Dr.*Shambhu* would be a suitable companion for *Antima*. He had a long conversation with *Antima*, who was quite reluctant to get into this wedlock. He somehow managed to convince her. Thus *Antima's* wedding with *Dr. Shambhu* was solemnized in a very simple manner. *Krishnendu* was unable to come down to India to attend his sister's wedding.

**_Marriage calls in for lots of mental adjustment:_** Getting married at the age of thirty, and entering into the joint family of the *Duttas*, was a new experience for *Antima*. Although she was quite mature, she was apprehensive whether she would be able to adapt and gel well with all the family members. Her father-in-law, *Shri Shankar Dutta*, was a learned and a renowned advocate of his times. He was quite jovial and talkative by nature. Her mother-in law, *Smt. Suhasini Dutta* was a person with strong likes and dislikes. She was a person who could not be easily satisfied. She was very fond of jewelry and saris. She was also a good cook. She was quite critical about *Antima's* complexion as she was not as fair as *Mitali*, *Shambhu's* first wife, and *Shefali*, her second daughter-in-law. Further, *Antima* was not from a rich family. She could not digest the fact that *Antima's* mother would be staying with her daughter in the *Dutta* family. However, since she had promised her husband and son that she would not raise this as an issue any further; she had to reluctantly accept *Antima's* mother's stay with her.

*Antima's* brother-in-law, *Shubhankar Dutta*, was five years younger than *Shambhu*. He was a Professor in Material Sciences in the Government Engineering College. His wife *Shefali* hailed from *Lucknow*, from a wealthy family. She was a trained Sitar player. She was quite impressed with *Antima's* academic achievement and her profession of teaching college students. Thereby she proved to be a good friend for *Antima*.

Her husband, *Dr. Shambhu Dutta* was a busy doctor. He was seen at home only during breakfast, lunch and supper. For a long time *Antima* and *Shambhu* communicated with each other in monosyllabic transaction. Both of them could not open up much as husband and wife. It was just a kind of contractual relationship; there was neither romance nor love that could blossom between them. *Antima's* father-in-law, *Shankar Dutta* did sense the situation and tried his best to bridge the gap. However, her mother-in-law, *Suhasini* often made it a point for her to realize that she could never take the place of *Mitali*, *Shambhu's* first wife. She was just an ornamental entity in the house labeled as a wife and a mother. Further, her mother living along with them became an opportunity for *Suhasini* to keep criticizing and casting aspersions on *Antima*. Thereby, the rosy picture of wedding proposal that was painted by her uncle, elder brother and her husband proved to be an illusion.

This was another cause of *Antima's* penetration into the quagmire of depression. Her brother-in-law sensed her state and asked his elder brother to take care of his wife. *Dr. Shambhu Dutta,* in turn asked her a few questions as a doctor does. There was no soulful conversation between them. Thus *Antima* from the age of 35 was put on anti-depression pills, without addressing and treating the root cause of her prevalent melancholic moods.

When *Antima,* came into the *Dutta* family, *Shishir* was a student of Class X and *Swagata* was studying in Class IV. *Shishir* was quite independent whereas *Swagata* needed help to organize herself, tending her hair and odd jobs. The ice started melting when she helped them out with their studies, projects, home tasks and assignments. In return, many a time, they amused *Antima's* mother with their talks and pranks. As they grew up *Sishir* became more like his father, he could never honour *Antima* as his mother, although *Swagata* was dependant and attached to her.

**Tragic deaths in the family:** One morning, on *Antima's* 45$^{th}$ birthday; *Mrunmayee* passed away in her sleep. *Antima* felt a void that none could fill.

Two decades after her wedding, when *Antima* was 50, fate took toll of three lives of the *Dutta* family. Dr. *Shambhu Dutta,* Advocate *ShankarDutta* and his wife *Suhasini* were returning from *Calcutta* by their Toyota driven by their driver, *Kailash*. A speeding truck collided and rammed into their vehicle from the front. Both the vehicles were at high speed on the highway. This led to the spot death of *Dr. Shambhu Dutta* and both the vehicle drivers. *ShriShankar Dutta* and *Suhasini* were critically injured. The former survived for 48 hours while the latter passed away after 56 hours. The shock was unbearable for everyone at home. Everyone was grief struck. *Antima* was now the widow of deceased, *Dr. Shambhu Dutta*.

*Shubhankar* performed the final rites for his parents, while *Sishir* performed the rites for his father. *Swagata* and *Sishir* were inconsolable. *Sishir* was now 35 and *Swagata* was 29. To the dismay of *Shubhankar*, *Shefali* and *Antima*; an announcement was made by *Sishir*.

He said, *"My sister Swagata and I will now onwards, no longer reside in this house belonging to my grandparents. We will be shifting to our maternal grandparents' Goswami family at Purulia"*.

*Sishir's* uncle, *Shubhankar* tried to cajole him and reason out, *"You are the heir to your father, isn't it your duty and your right to live in your paternal grandparents place?"*

*Sishir* replied, *"With the death of my father and my grandparents, I do not feel like living at this place. I have discussed with my maternal uncle and grandparents that we are going to shift to their place. So do not try to change my plans!"*

*Shubhankar* said, *"I am your 'kaaku', your paternal uncle and Shefali is your 'kaakimaa', don't we have the right to ask you to stay with us?"* He added, *"What about your maa? Will you leave her all alone?"*

*Shishir* looked at *Antima* with animosity and said, *"How can she be my mother? My 'maa' left for the heavenly abode when I and my sister were young! This lady can never take my mother's place! This lady had hoodwinked 'baaba' (father) to get into this house and acquire all our property."*

*Swagata* stood like a pole, without any kind of reaction or opposition to what her *'daada'* (elder brother) had said. *Antima* was stupefied and dumbstruck. She started trembling at *Sishir's* caustic remarks. She, for the first time realized that the children of *Dr. Shambhu Dutta* and *Mitali* had never accepted her as a member of the family; whereas she had always loved them as a mother does.

She announced tearfully in a sad voice, *"Sishir and Swagata, I may not be your biological mother, but I loved both of you truly and sincerely as a mother loves her children. Despite this fact, I realize today that I have no right to claim upon you as my children. So be it! God Bless You!"*

She addressed *Shubhankar* and *Shefali* and said, *"I am thankful to both of you that at least you two have rightfully addressed me as 'boudi' (eldest daughter-in-law)! Let Sishir and Swagata stay in this house of 'Dutta parivaar', I shall move out of this house, as I am the odd woman here. I shall claim no right on any kind of property or bank balance where I may have been nominated by my late husband. May I request you to kindly accommodate me for a fortnight. I shall move out as soon as I find a suitable accommodation or shelter for myself".* Antima tried her best to stay calm and composed. She could not.

She burst into tears as she moved out of the room. *Shubhankar* and *Shefali* tried their best to convince her but could not. On the other hand she thanked them profusely for their unconditional love and respect that they had been showering upon her for the past 20 years.

Thus, *Antima* moved out of the residence, wherein she had stepped in after she was wedded to *Dr. Shambhu Dutta*. She became a workaholic, always glued to teaching and research work. Since she was alone at home, she preferred to read a lot, extend her stay in the company of her colleagues and students. This happened until her retirement from her services as an English professor, when she was 62 years of age.

**Seeking solace:** Despite this, she often wondered at the vagaries of life. As a woman, she had proven her worth and mettle as a daughter and a sister; however she could never establish herself as a wife or a mother. She had lost everyone in her family, except *Krishnendu*, who was no doubt in touch with her; however she knew that he would never return to India. Would she be ever meeting Bimalenduda or *Arunimadi* at any point of time?

She expressed her gratitude to Almighty for having bestowed her with a school friend named *Sanchita*. Her friendship had helped her to be motivated and fight against her bouts and fits of depression. Her trip to *Jagannath Puri* was yet another step forward, seeking fulfillment in life. She could hear the following lines by *Sant Kabir Das* being sung as a *Bhajan*. This churned her soul! This is because it described the solace that *Antima* was seeking for! Here are the lines:

> **"मोकों कहाँ ढूँढे बंदे, मैं तो तेरे पास में।**
> **ना मैं देवल ना मैं मसजिद, ना काबे कैलास में।**
>
> **ना तो कौने क्रिया-कर्म में, नहीं योग बैराग में।**
> **खोजी होय तो तुरते मिलिहौं, पल भर की तालास में।**
> **कहैं कबीर सुनौ भई साथो, सब स्वाँसों की स्वाँस में।1**

"Where are you searching me for?
Oh follower! I am always with you.
Neither in pilgrimages; in statues; neither in solitude,
nor in temples, nor in the mosque,
Neither in the *Kaaba* nor in *Kailash*;
I'm with you, oh follower!
Neither in rituals or acts;
nor in communion or detachment!"
Sant Kabir addresses all the innocent ones in this quest,
"You could have surely found me within seconds of
search, within you;
for I live in every breath of yours"

\*\*\*\*\*\*\*\*\*\*\*\*\*\*\*\*\*\*\*\*\*\*\*\*\*\*\*\*\*\*\*\*\*\*\*\*\*\*\*\*\*\*

# GEMSTONES

# A Postlude to the Third Set of Stories

**Introduction:** Gemstones stand a class apart from pebbles and seashells, because of their lustre, brightness and sheen, when polished. Many of them when held against the sun reflect light that highlights the colour of the gemstone. Thereby, they are very much sought to by people and are cast intoornaments of various kinds. Here is a poem written the ABCEDARIAN style; wherein every line starts with the next letter of the alphabet and all letters from A through Zhave been included. I salute the poetess from Kansas (she writes in her profile the pen name of PinkFairie5) for having listed almost all the gemstones in the following verses.

### Gemstone Central

Amethyst, amber, agate, aquamarine; barite, bauxite, beryl, soon seen

Carnelian, chryophrase, cool citrine; diamond, dolomite, delivered by Dean

Emerald, epidite, elusive by far; fluorite flowing next to Feldspar,

Gemstone garnet hit parade, setting the bar and Hematite holds us hostage, said the Czar.

Isis calcite showing up imperial jade, Jasper enters the fray with his own maid.

Karats counted in diamonds, makes the grade; Lapis Lazuli, opens your third-eyea spiritual aid

Moonstone and malachite dancing in tune;Niccolite, and

nambulite against the moon
Opal and obsidian making fun of a rune; Pearl, pyrite, periodot doing a swoon.
Quartz comes up rosy, all pretty and pink.Ruby and rhodonite; sitting on the brink.
Sapphire, serpentine, sodalite sharing a drink; Topaz, tigers-eye and turquoise skating in the rink.
Attention now goes to uvite and unakite; making friends with vivionite and valencianite
Don't speak to wulfenite cautions wavelite. 'xtra dazzling, 'xtra special gemstones delight
Yeoperite says come meet *yowah*nut; Zeba jasper and zircon run right into the hut
These are not all the gemstones, but they are just a few. I would like to see a bit of each of them, now wouldn't you too?

**Usage of gemstones over various Ages in history:** Evolutionary history of manrecords that the oldest known gemstone jewelry was already madeby the *Neanderthals.*This is proven by archaeological findings made in south east Spain, in a cave. Archaeologists found shells with holes that were once studded with *hematite.*The oldest gemstones that were used werediamonds that dates back to 4.4 million years. In the Stone Age the gemstones that were used had to be easy to work with. Therefore amber (fossil resin), turquoise, coral, lapis lazuli and malachite were probably extensively used.

In the era of the ancient world Egyptian civilization, Greek and Roman Civilization as well as Indus Valley

Civilization, have testified the usage of gold and gemstones viz. emerald, ruby, opal and sapphire in crowns, headgears, crosses, diadems, decorative artifacts, necklaces, bracelets and armlets etc. Pearls were used as currency gems.

In the Middle Age period the magical properties of gemstones was acknowledged and thereby extensively propagated although precious stones were generally used to indicate and demonstrate status.

In the modern era, on the basis of scientific knowledge the processes of excavation, industries of mining, and large scale production of gemstones became technically sound. Gemstones were mainly used for their cosmetic value as well as applicative use. For e.g. diamond the hardest material was used in grinding industry especially steel and stone. Rubies were used in the very first lasers, in the early 1960s and are used by dermatologists. In addition to usage of gemstones as jewelry, they are extensively used for healing and spiritual practices, astrological based birthstones, decorative purposes and investment.

**The Indian belief of *Navaratna* (Nine Gemstones) and their importance:** In Vedic astrology it is believed that wearing the *Navaratnas* can bring positive energy and influence a person's life, by balancing the energies of planets in their respective astrological charts and bring good fortune.

**Planetary association of each gemstone:** Ruby / *Manikya* (Sun), Yellow sapphire / *Pukhraaj* (Jupiter), Blue

Sapphire / *Neelam* (Saturn), Emerald / *Panna* (Mercury), Diamond / *Heera* (Venus), Pearl / *Moti* (Moon), Precious Red Coral / *Moonga* (Mars), Hessonite Garnet / *Gomedh* (*Rahu*-Dragon's Head), Chrysoberyl Cat's eye / *Lehsunia* (*Ketu*- Dragon's Tail)

**Origin of gemstones, manufacture and marketing:** Gemstones are formed below the earth's surface. They may have sometimes traces of other minerals called inclusions. Diamonds and Zircon were formed deep in the Earth and brought to the surface by explosions of molten rock. Topaz, tourmaline and aquamarine, crystallized slowly from hot fluids and gases as they cooled and solidified, far below the surface of the earth. Others formed from liquids that filtered into cracks and pockets in the rock like the Australian opal. Some like garnet and jade formed when rocks were heated and pressurized by earth movements and recombined to form new, different materials. All gemstones, except pearls are of geological origin. Pearls are generated by the soft bodied molluscs termed as pearl oysters.

The variations of the following four Cs of gemstones viz. **carat, colour, clarity and cut** account for the market value of the gemstone.

**Human values versus gemstones:** We have often valued human beings as good souls / characters / Samaritans; based on their personality traits, character, behavioural traits, and values viz. passion, tenacity, integrity, service to mankind, leadership and benevolence etc. These are just a few traits of the innumerable human values. Such people are often referred to as **'gem of a person'.** Worldhistory and Indian history is bedecked with such personalities who have proven themselves as **'gems of personalities'** and have thereby become legendary and have added value to innumerable stories. Here are a few quotes followed by a couple of stories that highlight such gems and have inspired me to a great extent.

*"The world needs more gem-like people, who light up the darkness with their kindness."*

*"The best kinds of people are like precious gemstones, they bring out the beauty in others."*

*"In a world where everyone can be a pebble, it's a grant from providence to be a gem."*

*"A gem of a person is someone who uplifts others without expecting anything in return."*

*"A gem of a person is someone who leaves a lasting impact on others, an indelible mark in their hearts."*

\*\*\*\*\*\*\*\*\*\*\*\*\*\*\*\*\*\*\*\*\*\*\*\*\*\*\*\*\*\*\*\*\*\*\*\*\*\*\*\*\*\*\*\*\*\*

# The Solitary Septuagenarian

**Backdrop:** On 26 December 2004, the coasts of the *Andaman and Nicobar islands* experienced 10 m (33 ft) high tsunami waves following an undersea earthquake in the *Indian Ocean* which resulted in more than 2,000 casualties, 46,000 injuries and rendering at least 40,000 homeless. The locals and tourists on the islands suffered the greatest casualties while the indigenous people largely survived unscathed due to movement to high grounds following the oral traditions passed down over generations that warned them to evacuate following earthquake.

**Introduction:** This story is developed on the basis of the experiences of a journalist. *Sagar Neg*, the journalist from the Indian state of *Himachal Pradesh*, visited Port Blair in the year 2021, when India was celebrating the 75$^{th}$ Anniversary of its liberation and independence from British rule and occupation. On this occasion, India was organizing many events to promote its culture throughout the world, without forgetting to honour those who were tortured and lost their lives in the struggle for freedom. The freedom of the vast Indian country that had never invaded another country!

**Narration by *Sagar Negi* the Indian tourist journalist:** I reached Port Blair airport earlyin the morning on the 12$^{th}$ of August 2021; Thursday. I had booked my lodging and boarding at Hotel Ocean Terrace beach resort, which was a 20 minute drive from the airport. This was the first time that I had come down to *the Andaman and Nicobar Islands*. Thereby I had planned to stay along till the 17$^{th}$ of August, 2021. I was told by the driver that *Port Blair* is unusually crowded owing to the Independence Day Celebrations; otherwise the drive from the airport to the hotel should have taken only 10 minutes time. I was glad that the driver, *Abu Mohammed* could speak Hindi fluently. He was a *Keralite*, his grandfather, a coconut merchant had migrated to *Port Blair* soon after Independence; thereby he became a native of the islands.

I checked into the hotel room, located at the third floor. It was a large and spacious room. What impressed me most was the panoramic view that the large glass windows offered. It was the view of *Port Blair* harbour and jetty. There were quite a few residences around. I had a quick bath as I was quite tired after the car drive from *Dharamshala* to *Delhi* and the hop trip flights from *Delhi* to *Chennai* and *Chennai* to *Port Blair*. I sat on the window ledge of the hotel room, having a cup of hot tea and looked at all the view that I could see from that vantage point. The blue skies with a few fluffy white clouds, the horizon, and the vast blue ocean, the flight of birds, the palm groves, the six storey buildings and a few hutments as well.

As I was about having the last sip of tea; I was distracted below to the vast courtyard in front of a small thatched house, it had a flag fluttering on a pole at the centre of the courtyard. The white flag had the insignia of *Bharat Maata / Mother India* on a lion depicted with the map of undivided India. I had seen this photographic depiction of *Mother India*; however I wondered, that when we have an officially approved tricolour flag as designed by *Pingali Venkaiah* all over India, what does this flag depict / convey?

Meanwhile, the waiter came in to collect the tea-tray and accessories. I summoned him to the window and pointed out to the house with its front courtyard with the flagpole. I asked him if he had any idea about the flag, or the owner of the house. He replied that he had no idea at all.

It was around 10 a.m. I ventured out with my camera. I made a few enquiries at the reception. I walked out. I enjoyed the cool sea breeze as I walked out of the exit gate. I could not contain my curiosity about the hutment and flag on the flagpole. Thereby I narrated to the guard what I had seen and asked him the directions to the house that I had seen from the third floor of the Hotel. When the guard was told about the flag, he soon exclaimed, *"Saheb, who Mahatoji ka gharhai! Par Mahatoji abhi ghar par nahin milenge"* [*It's Mahtoji's residence, but he shall not be available at home*] I then asked him about *Mahatoji*. The guard spoke very high about him. He added, as he was on duty till 5:30 p.m. he would not be able to devote much time in narrating about him. After a while, he said that he would himself take me to *Mahatoji* and introduce me to him. He asked me to come down at 5:45 p.m. to the guard's station at the gate. I affirmed and went out walking to the main road.

It was wonderful sightseeing and clicking photographs as I had a photo-feature of the capital city of this island scheduled for the next issue of the weekly magazine titled *Reflections*. My major focus would be on the Cellular Jail, which I intended to next day as per my scheduled appointment. On the way, I found a photo-studio. I went in and checked for the availability of Kodak photo spools. Although I had a digital camera, I preferred the celluloid films that were always preferred by the printers for the print resolution. It took me an hour in the studio. I got acquainted with the shopkeeper *Mr. Randhir Pal* who had migrated from *Kolkata*.

It was around 1:30 p.m. I was quite famished. I was looking for vegetarian food joints as I was never accustomed to eggs, meat, fish, prawns and chicken that was abundant in majority of the hotels. A passer-by pedestrian, who was observing me, volunteered to help me out and directed me to a location on a street near a residential colony. This was a small attractive joint named *'Moussie ki Rasoi' (Aunt's kitchen)*. I was happy to see that *thali* (full plate) meal was being served with freshly made *rotis, fried dal,* mixed vegetable with gravy, fried ladyfinger, salad, rice and curd. The meal reminded me of the meal served by my mother at home.

*Smt. Amrita Sharma* was popularly known as *'moussie'* and she had started this venture of feeding *'shuddh shakahari bhojan'* [pure vegetarian meals] in this capital town. Her family hailed from *Lucknow*.

She was the daughter of *Pandit Jogeshwar Sharma* a freedom fighter sentenced to imprisonment (*Kaala Paani*) at the Cellular Jail during the British rule. He was one among the prisoners, who in 1932 started the hunger strike against the brutal behaviour of prison guards and the poor living conditions in the cells. The cellular jail prisons echoed with the cries of the prisoners who were subjected to mental and physical torture. Thereby, in May 1933, the strike took the shape of mass hunger strike that lasted for 45 days. The rebel prisoners were freed from these brutal conditions only in 1937 as an outcome of *Mahatma Gandhi* (who had made 17 consecutive hunger strikes) and *Rabindranath Tagore* reaching an agreement with the leader of the British colonial administration *Linlithglow* to release the prisoners. *Pandit Jogeshwar Sharma* was one among the last prisoners who were released in 1939.

After having a sumptuous meal, I preferred walking back to the hotel. On the way, I wondered at what I had read during school time about *Port Blair* in my History Text Book had subjected me as a child to associate and imagine that *Andaman & Nicobar Islands* was famous only for its tribal population and the Cellular Jail and *Kaala Paani sajaa* [rigorous out-of-sight imprisonment] during the British rule.

That is why I, probably dreaded the visit to the island on earlier opportunities. But what I was experiencing now was exhilarating! The pristine environment, the sea breeze, the sweet scent of flowers and herbs that floated in was indeed invigorating.

I walked to the Hotel and went into my room. It was 3:00 p.m. I sat down at the window ledge, stretching my legs and gazed at the view of the blue sky and the horizon. I did not realize when I fell asleep. When, I woke up it was quarter to five. I remembered that the guard had promised me to accompany me to *Shri Mahatoji's* hutment at 5:45 p.m.

I ordered for tea and browsed through the newspapers and magazines. The doorbell rang. It was the steward, who brought in the beverage that I had ordered for. I sipped the refreshing cup of tea and gazed at the harbour. I was once again distracted as I glanced at the hutment with the white flag of *Bharat mata* fluttering on the flagpole. The way the flag fluttered was indicative of the wind speed. At around 5:20 p.m. a gentleman clad in white *Punjabi Kurta* and a white Gandhi *topi* (Indian cap) came out. He had a frail body and was bespectacled. He tended to the potted plants around the flagpole. Sharp at 5:30 p.m. he went around the circular flagpole base thrice and saluted the flag. Soon after he brought down the flag, removed it from the rope to which it was attached. He tied the rope around the pole. He then folded the flag with reverence. He held the folded flag to his forehead for a while and then gazed at the sky. Then he walked inwards towards his hutment. The entire process took about 10 minutes.

It was 5:40 p.m. I quickly rushed out of the hotel room, went into the lift and got down to the reception, handed over my keys and walked to the guard, who was busy handing over his register and briefing the next guard to take charge of the post. He acknowledged my presence, with a big smile and whisked me out briskly by saying, *"Chaliye Saheb!"* We walked together, towards *Mahaoji's* hutment. I narrated to him, what I had witnessed at 5:30 p.m. and said, *"Mahatoji seems to be a devout Rashtrabhakt"/* (Devotee of the nation). *"Achhe Rashtra sewak bhi hain sahib"*, replied the guard. [*He is also a person who offers great service to the nation*]. We reached the hutment. The guard opened the gate and led me in through the long cobbled pathway. What I had seen as a small area from the top the hotel third floor, was actually quite a large area. We reached the door that was ajar. The guard knocked the door.

There was a voice from inside asking us to come in. The guard then said, *"Mahatoji, main Jitendra aaya hoon, aur ek sajjan ko bhi laaya hoon jo aapse milnaa chahte hain"* / ["Mahatoji, this is Jitendra, and along with me is a gentleman who aspires to meet you".]

To which, the voice replied, *"Aao Aao Jitendra, paanch minute lagenge, main jaldaaya, aap loag baitho!"/* ["*Come in Jitendra, I need five minutes, I shall come in soon, please be seated*"]

Meanwhile, I looked around the room. There were numerous black and white photographs on the wall. Each one showed *Mahatoji* in uniform. The room was neatly kept. There was a rifle hanging up on the wall. The large room otherwise appeared quite barren and empty. On the extreme left end was a huge walnut cupboard. The lower half had complete wooden doors while the upper half had glass doors. I could see through the glass doors three shelves. The topmost shelf had a display of accolades in the form of medals and trophies, the second shelf, had a display of mounted framed certificates, all bearing the name of *Limbaram Mahato,* in bold block letters.

After a short while, the frail looking person whom I had seen from the third floor of the hotel walked out, wiping his spectacles. He was now without his *topi.* He had jet black hair. He smiled at *Jitendra* the guard and accosted me, asking both of us to be comfortably seated on the sofa. Before *Jitendra* could speak, I plunged to begin the conversation by introducing myself and narrating the purpose of my visit to *Port Blair.* I also told him about the sight of the flag with the insignia of Bharat Mata, fluttering high on the flagpole in this premises that had caught my attention. This is what prompted me to come down to you. I thank my stars that I could meet the guard of the hotel, *Jitendra,* who was kind enough bring me in to your abode.

*Limbaram Mahato* smiled at me. He asked Jeetendra about his welfare. He looked at me and told me that he was touched by my curiosity. He also congratulated me for having come down to the capital city of Andaman & Nicobar Islands, for covering the 75$^{th}$ Independence Day Celebrations of our nation. He then questioned both of us, *"How old do you think am I?" Jitendra* replied in Hindi

"*Aap ki umra? Saath pain-sath tak hoagie*" [*Your age? It should be between 60 and 65*]. I did not say anything.

Then, *Limbaram Mahato* started narrating his story. "I am currently 76 years old. My father *Dulu Ram Mahato* was born in 1909, in a tribal village of West Bengal. He moved to his uncle's place at *Purulia* for his school education. As he grew older, he was greatly influenced by the writings of *Shri Aurobindo Ghosh*, the history behind the *Sepoy* Mutiny // Revolt of 1857, and the contribution by the following: *Ram Prasad Bismil, Bagha Jatin, Khudiram Bose, Ashfaqullah Khan, Sardar BhagatSingh, Chandrashekhar Azad, Subhash Chandra Bose, Bal Gangadhar Tilak, Sardar Vallabh Bhai Patel, Mahatma Gandhi* in the struggle for Indian Freedom. When at College, he joined the Bengal Volunteers // *Midnapore* Collegiate of Revolutionary activities.

Between 1931 and 1933, three young British District Magistrates of *Midnapore* (*Peddie, Douglas* and *Berge*) were assassinated in a row. In this context three were sentenced to death of each one's assassination; however there were many who suffered rigorous imprisonment i.e. *Kaala Pani Saja* at Port Blair, and my father *Dulu Ram Mahato* was one of them. He was then 24 years old.

Meanwhile, *Dulu Ram Mahato's* parents, uncle and wife had come to know about his secret deportation to *Port Blair*. They also decided to move in disguise to Port Blair. They did so stealthily with the help of fishermen who took them on board in a boat. They went on sail from *Kulpi* Port of West *Bengal* to *Port Blair*. They managed to be in the vicinity of the Cellular Jail, with the help of some fishermen and boatmen. *Limbaram Mahato* said, my father was released along with the last batch of prisoners in 1939. He was then 30 years old. Soon after a week *Dulu Ram Mahato* met his parents, uncle and wife.

I was born in 1945, six years later. Two years later, India got her Independence on 15th August 1947. My mother had narrated to me that it was *Bankim Chandra Chattopadhyay* who had in the 1870s painted Bharat Mata clad in saffron, dressed like a *sadhvi* (lady mendicant), with four hands one with a book, the other with paddy sheaves, third with a white cloth and the fourth with a rosary/*rudraksha* mala. Later in the year 1905, *Abanindranath Thakur*, nephew of *Rabindranath Tagore*, created the human form of Mother India / *BharatMata*. He titled it as *Matrimurti / BharatMata* in the magazine *Prabasi*.

By virtue of the system of rehabilitation of prisoners, we settled in a house. My father created the flag. It was he who drew *Bharat Mata* on a white cloth with the dimension of 3' x 2'. My mother painted it with natural dyes. He started the practice of daily hoisting it at dawn and lowering it at dusk, as a tribute to our motherland. The practice that my father began in 1939, I carry forward the same tradition in honour of our motherland and in memory of my father *Duli Ram Mahato*. Some observers regard this as a ritual. Some feel that when there is an official Indian tricolour, why I am continuing with the old model of the flag. This is to honour the past that was once the present and transited to the future (evolution of the flag). I respect the sanctity of this act in paying homage to our motherland before daybreak and nightfall.

My father started a school for young children who were poor and were not able to afford education. It was functional, initially in this very same hutment, where we are currently in. His efforts in running from pillar to post helped him in acquiring and allotment of a land and allocation of funds for this school. My father was successful in gathering like-minded people and establishing a model school for the poor and the destitute.

Currently I am 76 years young. I was fortunate to be trained by my father to be tough and strong. Right from the age of six he taught me to swim against tides in the sea, climb up heights with agility and run a marathon once in a week, rigorous physical training and breathing exercises. It was my father who often inspired me and motivated me by the stories and real life experiences.

Soon after Class XI School Finals, I joined the Border Security Forces, through written selection tests, physical fitness and endurance tests. I underwent a rigorous training. I joined in the artillery regiment as an Assistant Sub Inspector at *Farakka* Assam. After <u>five</u> years, I qualified and was promoted as Sub Inspector at *Punj*, Rajasthan, then after <u>four</u> years as an Inspector at West Bengal, followed by *Subedar* Major in the *Jammu* and *Kashmir* after <u>ten</u> long years. After rendering 19 years of service; I applied for voluntary retirement in 1980 which was granted. I returned to join my father at Port Blair and contributed to the development of the school. I introduced martial arts and developed a sports academy. I organised short term courses in archery, badminton, table tennis, volleyball, football, kho-kho and kabaddi, rifle shooting, chess, water surfing and skiing, folk music and folk dance. Children from an economically weaker background were greatly benefitted and have participated and excelled in National Games and Sports.

My father, *Duli Ram Mahato*, the freedom fighter, breathed his last in 1991. He was 82 years of age. He was my role model. It was he who motivated me to draw out the best from oneself and other citizens. Thus I became a true *Rashtrasewak*: a service oriented citizen of India, whom people today recognise as *Limbaram Mahatoji*.

It was on December 26, 2004, that I met the most challenging situation. This was when *Tsunami* struck the shores of *Andaman and Nicobar Islands*. I was surprised to find many of the tribal people, who were working in pastures, fields and countryside as well as at my school availing leave to flee away from the shore areas by 21$^{st}$ of December, 2004. Initially I presumed that the ones at school are trying to add more number of days to their Christmas break; however it was their indigenous konwledge that had prompted them to flee and escape the Tsunami.

Statistics reveals that more than 3.56 lakhs of people in 1089 villages of Andaman and Nicobar Islands was affected.*Limbaram Mahato*, pooled in a team of 150 local volunteers who were mainly engaged in rescuing people, retrieving people and dead bodies, identification and proper disposal of dead bodies along with restoration of essential infrastructure, transport and telecommunications. Majority of the retrieved people were accommodated at 10 nodal centres and one of them was their school building; which was partially destroyed. The major issues were availability of drinking water, food packets and clothing. The para-military forces that were deployed sought the help of local people for delving into areas that were worst hit.

Although *Limbaram Mahatoji's* contribution to the relief and rescue process along with the Para Military forces was recognised and rewarded by the Government; he still dreads that day as he had failed in rescuing quite large numbers of people.

*Sagar Negi* was awestruck listening to the mammoth efforts of the solitary septuagenarian. He felt that the first day of his trip to Port Blair was quite fulfilling! Here is a couplet / *doha* by Sant *Kabir*:

## बडा हुआ तो क्या हुआ जैसे पेड़ खजूरा
## पंथी को छाया नही फल लागे अति दूर ॥

(*Badaa*) Huge / Big; (*Hua toh kya hua?*) what's the use? (*jaise paed khajur*) like the date palm trees; (*Panthi ko chhaya nahin*) provides no shade to the travelers; (*Phal laage ati dur*) Fruits are borne at a distance

It is no use being very big or rich if you cannot do any good to others. The Palm tree is undoubtedly tall, yet it is of no use to a traveller as it neither provides shade nor are the fruits easily available as they are located quite high in the tree.

\*\*\*\*\*\*\*\*\*\*\*\*\*\*\*\*\*\*\*\*\*\*\*\*\*\*\*\*\*\*\*\*\*\*\*\*\*\*\*\*\*\*\*\*\*\*\*\*\*\*\*\*\*\*

# *The Navaratna Pendant*

**Introduction:** It was 3rd October 2021; the *Shetty* family was busy planning organising the ninth birthday celebrations of *Minnie*, the daughter of *Mrs. & Mr. Govind Shetty* which was scheduled for the next day. The *Shettys'* had a huge mansion at the heart of *Panaji*, the capital of Goa. This mansion was constructed by *Mr. Govind Shetty's* father, *Shri Krishna Shetty* in 1950.

The venue for the birthday celebrations was the plush lawns surrounding the aquamarine blue pool. The event management group named as *Party Pulse* was entrusted the responsibility for the grand birthday celebrations. About twemty of their personnelswere engaged in decorating on the theme of Seashells. A pair of huge sea-horses flanked the gate. From this point, one could see a pathway made of artificial material that resembled seashells. The stage that was erected had a backdrop of a sea beach with a variety of 3D seashells.

*Mr. Govind Shetty* was a renowned industrialist in Goa. *Mr. Govind Shetty* was an M. Tech in Polymer Sciences and thereby he was the Director cum Chairman of Polymer industry. This unit was responsible for the production of flexible packing material using rayon and synthetic fibres. Although he lived in North Goa; he had his chain of flourishing business in important places in both North and South Goa.

*Govind Shetty's* father *Shri Krishna Shetty* had taken on lease from the Portugese, the mining industries that dealt with extraction of iron ore, manganese and mica. The petition No. 435/2012, led to the Supreme Court passing its famous order of 5$^{th}$ October 2012, disallowing the restart of any mining activities in Goa and injuncting anyone in the State trading or transporting mineral ores. This unprecedented development brought in heavy losses. *Shri Krishna Shetty*, who had a roaring business once upon a time, was so dejected that he moved out from industry and shifted to agriculture in his native village near *Hubli, Karnataka*. *Krishna Shetty's* elder son, *Madhusudhan Shetty* diverted his father's business of mining to alluvial sand mining industry. His younger brother, *Gopal Shetty* was the Director of a pharmaceuticals company.

The three brothers, each one's wife and children, all of them lived together in the mansion. Eldest brother, Mr. *Madhusudhan Shetty's* wife, *Shobhana* was a graduate of her times. She had taken full charge of the mansion after her mother-in-law moved out with her father-in-law to their native village near *Hubli*. She was a mother of two. The elder son, *Sharath*, was studying in Boston. The younger daughter, *Shamita*, was pursuing a course in fashion designing from *Karavalli* institute at *Mangalore*.

Mr. *Govind Shetty's* wife, *Darshana* was an educated lady from *Mengaluru*, who was very interested and creative in textile designing and cosmetic jewellery designing. *Minnie* was born six years after their wedding. Mr. *Gopal Shetty's* wife, *Bhawana* had completed her Ph.D. in Chemistry from *Ferguesson College, Pune*. She worked with her husband in his factory as an Assistant Director. She had a daughter named *Aradhya* who was in Class VIII and a son named *Aditya* in Class V in a reputed school at *Panaji*.

All the family members, including all the children and grandparents *Mrs. Kamini Shetty* and *Mr. Krishna Shetty* had come down to attend *Minnie's* ninth birthday celebration.

In the mansion there lived eight staff members. Two of them were responsible for taking care of the following pets: a pair of cockatoos named *Pepper* and *Smiley*. There were five dogs all of different breeds, named after planets *Pluto* the bull dog, *Neptune* the cocker-spaniel, *Jupiter* the Alsatian, *Uranus* the German Shepherd and *Venus* the Pomeranian. There were eight cats named *Poppy, Misty, Charlie, Simba, Tabby, Brownie, Shadow and Toby*. It's quite vivid from this that the *Shetty* family loved to have pets.

**4$^{th}$ October 2021, Minnie's birthday:** *Minnie* woke up earlier than usual. It was a Monday morning. She had a bath. She wore the traditional dress of '*pattupaavada-sokkai*' [silk long skirt and blouse] which was gifted to her by her mother. She went to the room of her grandparents. They were already up as they were early risers. Their biological clock was set to waking up at 4:30 a.m. daily. They would always advise their grandchildren to wake up at this hour of *brahmamuhurta*.

They were happy to see *Minnie* in the new traditional attire. They asked her to come in. She touched the feet of her grandparents and they blessed her. Grandfather/*ajja* gifted a set of nine illustrated story books on great women of the country. The titles were *Abakka Chouta, Bhima bai Holkar, Rani Chennamma of Kittur, Jhansi Rani Lakshmi Bai, Begum Hazrat Mahal, Rani Durgawati, Velu Nachhiyaar, Madam Bhika ji Cama, Kamaladevi Chattopadhyay.*

Meanwhile, grandmother/*ajji* took out a small and attractive red coloured brocaded satin drawstring bag and gifted it to her grand daughter *Minnie*. She could not resist her curiosity. She immediately opened the drawstring loose and delved into the bag. She drew out a circular box of 6 inch diameter with a transparent lid. She opened it and found a golden chain with a circular pendant studded with nine gemstones. *Ajji* was happy to see the brightness in *Minnie's* eyes.

Ajji said, *"As it's your ninth birthday, I decided to gift you the Navaratna; a combination of nine gemstones. The best form that I could present to you these nine gems would be a gold pendant / locket mounted with all the nine gemstones."* Minnie was overwhelmed. She put on the chain with the *Navaratna* pendant and looked at herself in the large mirror. She adjusted the chain such that the pendant hung right at the centre. She profusely thanked both *ajja* and *ajji* and went out of the room, richer by a golden chain with a navaratna pendant and the lifestoriesogf nine valorous women of India.

*Minnie* ran to the room of her parents (*tande* & *taayi*), quite excited with her grandparents' gifts. She displayed them to her parents and touched their feet as well. She received the blessings from her parents. They announced that the gift meant for her ninth birthday would be given to her in the evening during the birthday party; thereby she had to hold her breath of surprise until then. *Govind and Darshana said to Minnie, "Let's go to the temple, It's nice to see that you have had your bath and are ready."* Thus all the three of them moved out in their vehicle to the *Mahalakshmi* temple, quite a popular deity of the city and locality.

By the time all the rituals were over at the temple it was 9 a.m. Although *Minnie* had applied for leave she wanted to meet her School Principal and teachers on this day, her birthday and seek their blessings. *Darshana said, "But we haven't brought any sweets for them". "Amma didn't I tell you that our school does not permit distribution of confectionaries. I have brought this box with 50 seed balls; one each for my 35 classmates and remaining for the School Principal, Vice Principal and teachers. My classmates shall plant the seed ball in their respective gardens or clay pots and take care of them. When they see the plant grow, I shall be blessed. The same applies for the School Principal and Staff."*

*Govind* was amused to overhear their conversation. He drove the car to the School. At school everybody greeted *Minnie*. The *Navaratna* pendant that she was wearing caught the attention of almost every one. Her friends went gaga over it. The School Principal gifted a pen, while the teachers blessed her.

146

While returning, her father remarked, *"Minnie your pendant is beautiful indeed. It was vey thoughtful of your grandma to have gifted you such a beautiful talisman on your ninth birthday! Be careful! Never lose it!"* When they returned home it was almost 10 a.m. They found the decoration by event management group -*Party Pulse* quite unique and almost on the verge of completion.

*Minnie* sought the blessings of from her *Doddappa, Doddamma, Chikappa and Chikkamma*. Both her uncles and aunts blessed her and gifted a set of pearl jewellery. Her cousins wished her by singing in chorus the song...... HAPPY BIRTHDAY and each one of them fed her with a spoonful of '*payasam*' [Indian dessert made of milk, sugar and rice, laced with cardamom powder and dry fruits].

The *Navaratna* pendant that hung from the gold chain and was seated on *Minnie's* chest caught the attention of everyone. Their eyes brightened as they saw the sparkling gemstones. *Shobhana* and *Bhawna* kept feeling both the sides of the pendant and remarked, *"Beautiful workmanship! Amma always has a good eye and taste for finesse and craftsmanship.... Minnie you are lucky that you have got this piece of jewellery as a gift from Amma on your 9th birthday. Keep this gift from your ajji safe till your 90th birthday!"*

*Pepper* and *Smiley* wished *Minnie* in their cockatoo voices by repeatedly screeching *"appybudday!"*. *"appybudday!"*.... *"appybudday!"* On hearing the cockatoos screech, the dogs started growling and the cats raised their tails and started mewing. Everyone started laughing.

*Sharath* handed over *Minnie* a box of chocolates and said, *"These chocolates are straight from Boston, You'll surely love them."* *Shamita* gave her a set of cosmetic jewellery. *Aradhya* and *Aditya* gifted a set of books on papercraft and a musical keyboard.

The grandparents and their three sons had retired soon after lunch. There was a lot of merriment and rejoicement till 3 p.m. *Shobhana*, *Darshana* and *Bhawna* shooed the children away to their respective rooms such that they could rest and be ready by 5 p.m. as the invitees and guests to the evening party were expected by 6:30 p.m.

On this occasion of *Minnie's* birthday; the eight staff members of the house were specially fed by the ladies of the house. The five pet dogs had a special cereal with chicken-sticks while the cats had a meal of cooked unseasoned chicken, fish and eggs. As they had the meal, the pet dogs whimpered and whined while the pet cats trilled and purred. The gist of their communication was, *"Praise the human beings! Praise them that we are their pets! Happy Birthday Minnie! We wish that we are born as human beings in our next lives!"*

*Minnie*, the birthday girl was ready by 6 p.m. The music by Party Pulse was on in a loud volume. *Minnie* had adorned herself in a maroon coloured calf length frock with full sleeves and floral appliqué work running diagonally from the left shoulder to the right waist. She had curled up her long hairs and had a beautiful tiara on her head; the stones of which sparkled. The chain with the *navaratna* pendant did not go well with her party dress. She wanted to remove the chain off, however she could not. She called for her mom.

Her mom was busy supervising the staff that was busy shifting the dogs from their kennels and the cats from the cattery (that were located in the pool side lawns) into the hall at the rear end. This was a measure taken to ensure that the animals would not start yelping or snarling on listening to the loud music and the hubbub by so many strangers and guests around.

*Minnie* was in a hurry. She walked to her mother, *Darshana*. Her *amma* understood her problem and asked her to turn around, such that she could easily spot the catch / hook of the chain. As *Darshana* was busy locating the catch which was at the nape of *Minnie's* neck; the lights suddenly went off and the music stopped playing.

It was quite dark, however *Uranus*, the German Shephard got excited spotting *Minnie* and he broke lose and jumped at her from behind. *Minnie* felt a tug at the nape of her neck and could feel the golden chain with the *navaratna* pendant slipping from her neck. Her mom, *Darshana* had one end of the chain in her palm. She kept shouting, *"What's happened to the lights? Switch on the lights!"*.

The pet dogs and cats could see well in this darkness. The dogs aped their mate *Uranus* in getting free from their master's hands. Meanwhile the pendant studded with gemstones fell on to the ground, distracting *Uranus*. The German Shephard caught the pendant by its right forepaw. The hook of the pendant was sharp that *Uranus* kicked the pendant ahead. It was now the turn of *Pluto*, the bull dog to jump on the pendant and cover it by both the legs. After a while it kicked the pendant to *Jupiter*. What was kicked by *Jupiter* was caught by *Neptune* who in turn passed it on to *Venus*. It was as though all the five pet dogs were engaged in playing a relay of striking wherein the pendant was the striker. The two staff members, who were in charge of the dogs and cats, could not make out the cause of excitement among the dogs. Coincidentally, none of them had brought their cellphones with them, so that they could have switched on the torchlights in the device.

On sensing that the dogs were playing among themselves; the cats became alert. *Poppy* signalled to *Misty*. *Misty* had noticed something shiny being passed on to *Venus*; thereby she focused her eyes and raised her ears. *Charlie and Simba* noticed Misty's signal and they pounced on the pomeraraian *Venus*. She ran from her spot leaving the shining pendant to the mercy of *Tabby* and *Brownie*. They were initially scared to see the golden disc. As both of them developed the guts to handle the circular object; the lights were on! Meanwhile, *Shadow* and *Toby* jumped upon *Brownie* and *Tabby*. In this process the circular pendant was lifted up to a height and fell down by its rim to roll down the length of the hall to a crevice in the corner. *Shadow, Tabby, Brownie* and *Toby* dashed behind the object but they were confused as they could not find the object.

As soon as the lights were on; *Minnie* and her mother realised that the *navaratna* pendant had fallen off the chain which was in her hand. They frantically searched for the pendant, without informing others or raising an alarm. *Minnie* started weeping. *Darshana* glanced at her wrist watch and realised that it was 6:15 p.m. She took *Minnie* to the corner of the hall, asked her to wipe off her tears and consoled her. She added, *"Let this be between you and me, do not disclose anything about the missing pendant to anyone. 'Ajji' will feel bad if she comes to know about the pendant that she had so fondly gifted you. I will handle the matter."*

This was when Minnie's *appa* entered with a brand new bicycle that was delivered by the stores then. He said, *"This is your birthday gift that I had mentioned to you in the morning as your surprise gift!"* Govind Shetty on the other hand was surprised to see that his daughter did not show any kind of response. He grew concerned and asked if anything was wrong. *Minnie* would have burst into tears and would have told her father about the missing pendant; however she gathered herself and hugged him and said, *"Thank You Appa! This is the same brand of bicycle that I had aspired for!"* Her father was relieved at her response.

People started pouring in large numbers. Friends, relatives and guests, all had come in to bless *Minnie* on her birthday. People enjoyed the events that were organised by Party Pulse for children, youngsters, adults and senior citizens. The atmosphere was charged up with music and beats to which people started spontaneously tapping their feet.

At 8:30 p.m. *Minnie* was led by *Ajja, Ajji, Doddappa, Dodamma, Appa, Amma, Chikkaappa, Chikkamma* and all her cousins for the Cake Cutting Ceremony. *Govind Shetty* profusedly thanked all the invitees for having blessed his daughter by their gracious presence on the occasion of his daughter's ninth birthday on his invitation. He asked all of them to join for dinner. *Minnie* was undoubtedly happy and overwhelmed. However the 'missing *navaratna* pendant' kept haunting her.

The party was over by 11 p.m. By the time the dinner was over for all at *Shetty's* mansion, it was midnight. All folks in the mansion had retired by 12:30 p.m. The pets: cockatoos, cats and dogs were kept in the hall at the rear end as it was too late to shift them to their cage, kennels and cattery.

At 1:00 p.m. *Uranus* who was sleeping woke up sniffing. He smelt something strange. He stretched his legs and got up and started following the trail of scent. At his movement all the other four dogs also woke up and started observing the movement of *Uranus*. The cats also stirred from their sleep. *Poppy, Misty, Charlie and Simba* woke up when they sensed a small rodent's claws upon them. They were startled to discover that it was a rat that had scurried upon them. All the four chased the rat that *Uranus* had sniffed. The rat was faster than all all the five of them. It outwitted them as it was always ahead as it briskly scampered all over the hall.

Finally it reached the crevice where the pendant had rolled in earlier in the evening, and vanished into thin air. *Shadow, Tabby, Brownie* and *Toby* gathered near the crevice and started inserting their forepaws into the crevice. As a result the concrete around the crevice (junction edge at the base of the wall and the floor) which probably had lots of sand in proportion to lime gave away and resulted in a big hole, which led to a tunnel. The tunnel must have been definitely created by rodents.

The cats started meowing in tune when they were unable to move out into the tunnel as the rat hole was too small for them to move out. The cockatoos stirred in their places and screeched aloud when they heard the chorus of meows! The staff members were too tired to wake up and look into the cause of commotion. Meanwhile the visiting rodents had dragged the pendant into the tunnel while they scurried out.

Next day morning, *Darshana Shetty* made it a point to wake up earlier than usual and examine thoroughly the rear end of the hall in search of the missing *Navaratna* pendant. It was her gut feeling that the pendant must have fallen there alone when the lights had suddenly gone off due to power disruption. She was surprised to observe the faecal matter of rodents at one end of the hall. She asked one of the the staff to carefully broom and mop the floor.

In this process she was terrified to find a rat-hole in the corner. She asked the staff to insert a ladle into the rat hole and scoop out all that was possible. She asked another staff to stand out in the garden opposite to the hole to ensure how far the ladle was able to scoop out the mud. This person suggested that following the trail of the ladle if we could carefully dig out the mud, it's quite possible that it would be rewarding.

*Darshana* found some logic in his suggestion and asked the gardener to help him out in digging along the pathway of the loose soil that the rodents had thrown up while tunnelling. After a length of one and half feet, the gardener found quite a lot of things inside the tunnel viz. an eraser, a sharpener (*Aditya* had lost weeks ago), cigarette butts, discarded button cells, decorative pebbles and marble stones, thermocol balls and unbelievably after half an hour the missing pendant was seen.

*Darshana* who had lost all hopes, she cried out with joy on observing the pendant lying partially buried in the soil! She patted herself that she had taken the right decision to search for the pendant instantly as soon as she she woke up that day, rather than completely losing hopes.

This reminded her of Sant Kabir's couplet that she had read in *Minnie* and *Aditya's* Hindi Text Book on avoiding procrastination and postponing thoughts:

**काल करे सो आज कर, आज करे सो अब।
पल में परलय होएगी, बहुरि करेगा कब।**

*(Kaal Kare)* Actions for tomorrow; *(Aaj kar)* Do them today; *(So Ab)* Do them now; *(Pal Mein)* in a moment; *(Parlay)* Disaster; *(Hoyegi)* will happen; (***Bahuri karega kab?***) when will you find time for all actions?

"Do not keep overthinking and postponing your actions. Be prompt enough to do the work that needs to be done now. There could be a disaster any moment. Therefore do not lose time."

She ran to her daughter's room and shook her up from her deep sleep. Initially *Minnie* could not decipher why her mother was shaking her up so viglrously. She groaned and grumbled. But when her mother held out her palm with the pendant that she had lost on the previous day, she forgot her sleep and cried with joy! *Minnie* hugged her mother to express her gratitude!

\*\*\*\*\*\*\*\*\*\*\*\*\*\*\*\*\*\*\*\*\*\*\*\*\*\*\*\*\*\*\*\*\*\*\*\*\*\*\*\*\*\*\*\*

www.ingramcontent.com/pod-product-compliance
Lightning Source LLC
LaVergne TN
LVHW041948070526
838199LV00051BA/2949